Party
DISASTER!

Party Disaster!

SUE LIMB

BLOOMSBURY

LONDON BERLIN NEW YORK SYDNEY

Bloomsbury Publishing, London, Berlin, New York and Sydney

First published in Great Britain in June 2012 by Bloomsbury Publishing Plc
50 Bedford Square, London, WC1B 3DP

A CIP catalogue record for this book is available from the British Library

ISBN 978 0 7475 9918 0

Typeset by Hewer Text UK Ltd, Edinburgh
Printed in Great Britain by Clays Ltd, St Ives plc, Bungay, Suffolk

1 3 5 7 9 10 8 6 4 2

www.bloomsbury.com
www.JessJordan.co.uk

For Darcy Alexandra Meyers

Chapter 1

Jess sat in her bedroom and wrote a title on a piece of paper: Reasons to Be Cheerful. *There have to be some*, she thought desperately. Life had been beastly recently, with Fred behaving – well, behaving like a rat. So what *did* she have to be cheerful about?

Jess stared moodily at the carpet. A tiny beetle ran under her desk. Luckily she didn't mind insects. Just rats, really. Especially the human sort.

1) I'm not a cockroach. A bit of a random reason to be cheerful, but she had to start somewhere. Although it's possible, admitted Jess, that cockroaches have a lifestyle that's one hundred per cent fun, holding raves on the floors of dirty kitchens every night of the year.

2) I'm not obese. During the winter, thick fleeces had kept her bod discreetly veiled, but now spring was

here and she was going to have to foist her lard on the unsuspecting public. Her backside was so big, she often had the feeling she was being followed.

3) I'm not seriously ill. Jess paused. She'd better check first. She started by examining her hands. They looked just about OK – at least they hadn't fallen off in the night. Jess became distracted by her fingers. She'd read somewhere that having an index finger shorter than your ring finger meant that you might have some masculine characteristics, such as being good at maths and asserting yourself. Jess sighed. Her index finger was definitely longer than her ring finger, so it was unlikely that she would turn out to be a stylish mathematician with her own TV game show.

4) My mum and dad, though divorced, are friends. Her parents had got divorced when she was too young to remember any of it. Though mad in their own quiet ways, they were so well behaved they'd probably managed not to throw too many plates at each other. If any china had been hurled, it was most likely only egg cups.

5) Granny understands me and is still alive (that is, she was when I last looked). Jess suddenly had a horrid thought and raced downstairs. Granny was sitting in front of the TV, fast asleep with her mouth open. Jess stared

anxiously at Granny's chest encased in its cosy hand-knitted cardi emblazoned with a woolly picture of dolphins leaping joyfully in and out of a blue-green sea. Thank goodness! The sea was rising and falling regularly, an infallible sign that Granny was still alive, though Jess did feel a slight pang of seasickness. On the TV somebody was being ill treated by an alien. Granny found sci-fi and horror delightfully soothing. Though tempted to stay and watch the earth being saved from the brink yet again, Jess ran back upstairs. She still hadn't thought of a reason to be really cheerful, something that cancelled out all the annoying stuff.

6) I've never been tortured by aliens. In fact, being tortured by your very own friends was worse, as Jess now realised. She sighed and stared up at her bulletin board. It was adorned with random stuff: photos of terriers skateboarding, some pics of Flora mugging at the camera, trying to pull a horrendous face yet somehow remaining almost illegally beautiful . . . There were no images of Fred. (Nor of his latest flame, the unstoppable, indestructible, shameless Jodie.) They'd all been stashed away in Jess's wardrobe. At the thought of Fred, a wave of rage and indignation swept through her.

Jess grabbed a pencil and ripped a piece of blank paper off a pad. She drew a cartoon of Fred, exaggerating his long legs, his short bristly hair, his huge eyes. Next to him she drew a cruel caricature of Jodie, much fatter than she'd ever been in real life, and dolled up in a bride's veil. Above the happy couple, Jess wrote in red felt tip, You may kick the bride! Then she pinned it to her bulletin board. *I must get some darts*, she thought. Firing some arrows off at that irritating pair would cheer her up in her worst moments.

Reluctantly she dragged herself away from the wedding pic of Fred and Jodie, and returned to her Reasons to Be Cheerful. She really did want to be cheerful again, not kind of smouldering from an inner fire the way she had been for weeks now.

7) I'm lucky to live in the age of TV. Imagine all those poor Stone Age people, forced to draw mammoths on cave walls to while away the time. And how did they even play charades in the prehistoric era? You couldn't start with 'Is it a book, a film or a movie?' It would always have to be a cave painting, an odd-looking vegetable or a lump of mammoth poo that looked amusingly like somebody's head.

8) Despite humanity's attempts to ruin the planet, we still have small, furry, cuddly animals. *Just not in this actual house*, thought Jess resentfully. Despite a relentless campaign of nagging, she was as far away from

having a pet as ever. The nearest thing she had to a small fluffy creature was her fur-trapper's hat which was made of polyester. Maybe it should be known as a polyester-trapper's hat. She was quite tempted sometimes to call it Twinkle and to take it for walks on a lead.

9) I'm not going out with Luke. Although Luke was a really lovely guy, and amazingly talented, for Jess to go out with him would have been wrong, wrong, wrong. She had made the right decision there, at least.

At this point Jess sighed and threw away her pen. She had meant to toss it lightly on to the desk and for it to lie there creating an atmosphere of chic despair. Instead it bounced off the wall and fell down behind the back of the desk. She glared at the cartoon of Fred and Jodie getting married. It gave her a strange, ferocious pleasure. She thought she might do some more drawings of them later. She might invent some horrible children for them, and a vile dog called Frodie who looked a bit like Jodie. And she'd make them live in a nasty house covered with house-warts.

This bitter and twisted mood had to be dispelled somehow. Jess tried to pull herself together. She decided to do the only sensible thing: flip open her laptop, find a tarot website and get an instant reading.

She was immediately instructed to *think of a question or an object of concern*. Jess closed her eyes. *How much longer am I going to have to endure this?* she begged the invisible Fates. *Will things ever get back to the way they were?*

She'd selected a three-card reading – for the past, present and future. The first card to be revealed represented the past. It was the Five of Swords and symbolised Loss and Regret. 'Too right!' cried Jess aloud. She read on. *Sometimes one has to accept one's errors in judgement and one's rash and belligerent actions.* But had she made an error in judgement?

She looked up *belligerent* in the online dictionary just in case it might mean something not quite as bad as she suspected. *Inclined or eager to fight*, the definition said. *Hostile or aggressive*. She wondered whether she had been hostile or aggressive, or whether she'd been perfectly justified when she let rip at Fred during Chaos, the Valentine's dinner dance.

Abandoning the online tarot reading in despair, Jess went downstairs. Granny had woken up from her little nap and was watching avidly as a Special Space Force Agent destroyed some aliens without, miraculously, ruining her hair.

'She's got them on the run now,' Granny commented

reassuringly. 'But there's a twist right at the end – they've taken over her partner's body. I've seen this one before.'

'What happens in the end?' asked Jess, flopping down on the hearthrug beside Granny's feet.

'It's one of those coat hanger episodes,' said Granny. 'Cliffhanger, I mean. She finds her mate again and there's this grand reunion, but gradually she realises that he's been taken over by an evil alien force.'

Jess shuddered with recognition. Something very similar had been happening in her own life, ever since Fred had started going out with Jodie.

Chapter 2

'Granny,' said Jess, 'my life is in ruins.'

'Join the club, dear,' murmured Granny, still staring at the TV screen. 'Whose isn't?'

Quite frankly, Jess was disappointed at this reply – from her grandmother of all people. Granny baked cakes. She did tapestry. She even wore hand-knitted cardis. Where was the sympathy? Where were the cuddles? Had Granny, too, been taken over by aliens?

'Sorry . . .' Granny reluctantly dragged her eyes away from the TV. The credits were rolling now, so she wasn't missing anything. 'What were you saying?'

'My life is in ruins.'

'Why?' demanded Granny, her head cocked on one side, looking like a fluffy little bird.

'Well, you know I dumped Fred. And then he started going out with Jodie.'

'Jodie . . .' Granny looked thoughtful. 'Is she that pretty girl with the lovely smile?'

That pretty girl with the lovely smile? Jess felt shocked that Granny hadn't described Jodie as that scheming so-and-so with the awful acne, muffin-top and a voice that could curdle custard. Jess had to admit that Jodie had slimmed down recently – she and Fred had embarked on a fitness regime training for a half-marathon in aid of charity. Her skin had improved. Her hair looked shinier. Flora had once remarked that Jess and Jodie were similar in some ways. Her exact words had been, 'You know, sometimes I think Jodie is a tubby, low-budget version of you.' Now it was almost the other way around.

'You can do better than Fred,' said Granny with a contented sigh, picking up her tapestry (she was creating a cushion cover of Elvis, her heart-throb from when she was a teenager). 'You don't want to settle down now anyway. You're far too young.'

I bet Granny would have settled down with Elvis if he'd been available whatever her age, thought Jess venomously. She picked irritably at the hearthrug. Although she was still very annoyed with Fred, she didn't want to hear Granny dissing him. 'I definitely don't want to settle down too early and all that gubbins. But I'm not sure I *could* do better than Fred. Even if he is barely human.'

'Why did you dump him, then?' asked Granny sharply.

Jess sighed. 'He was totally spineless,' she explained. 'When we were trying to organise that Valentine's dinner dance and everything went wrong, he just left me in the lurch. And then on the night he upstaged me in what was supposed to be *my* hosting routine. You remember, Granny – I told you all about it!'

'Well, I think you can do much better than a spineless boy who leaves you in the lurch and upstages you,' said Granny. 'As you know, dear, I think that Luke from next door is a lovely boy. But if you really do want to win Fred back, it's simple. All you have to do is become marvellous. Any other problems?'

'No.' Jess shrugged. She silently vowed never to talk to Granny about Fred again. Granny was supposed to remind her of all Fred's wonderful qualities, not join in the whingeing about his lack of vertebrae.

'Now that's settled, go and put the kettle on, dear,' said Granny quickly, as if she was glad to be shot of the subject, 'and make me a cup of tea.'

Jess hauled herself heavily to her feet and sloped off

to the kitchen. Granny seemed a bit sharp today. What Jess really craved at the moment was oodles of sympathy. Granny should have leapt up off her chair and run to the kitchen herself, insisting upon making Jess a cup of hot chocolate. Actually, why stop there? What she longed for was a chocolate cake. And a dress made of chocolate. In fact, if Granny had any sympathy for Jess's troubles, she should coat the whole house in chocolate so Jess could spend the rest of the week licking the walls.

Instead it was she, Jess, the tragically suffering one, who had to endure the endless journey to the kitchen, then, when she arrived, she had to switch the light on – yes, actually raise her arm to the light switch and, with all her puny strength, press downward. Had her wicked grandmother no pity at all?

She filled the kettle, switched it on, got out two mugs and two tea bags – no, wait! Tea bags weren't good enough for Her Highness Lady Grandma Muck. It had to be proper loose tea in a warmed pot. Would the tea-making torment never end? Jess found the teapot, which was still full of old, cold stewed tea left there by some feckless, useless, lazy person. Then she had to tip out the tea bags and squeeze them. Disgusting! In any decent home that job would not have to be done by the young princess. There would be a special servant waiting outside the back door to squeeze tea bags – indeed, to do all disgusting and boring chores. His name would be Woebegone.

Then she had to warm the pot! Jess ground her teeth in rage. She was not born to warm pots. She had come into this world to do beautiful, dazzling, astonishing things. But here was her wicked grandmother demanding that she warm pots. Jess waited until the kettle had boiled – oh, an endless wait! – and then poured a bit of boiling water into the pot.

I expect I shall spill a bit now and burn my hand, thought Jess. *Then the skin will fall off, and children will poke fun at me in the street and shout, 'The Hideous Hand! The Hideous Hand!' and run off, screaming.*

She didn't scald herself, as it turned out, but surely it was only a matter of time. She waited while the pot warmed up beneath its stupid lid. Then she tipped out the water and switched the kettle back on. Three spoonfuls of Granny's loose tea – 'Orange Pekoe, dear, always. Nothing else will do!' – then she poured on the boiling water. It made a faint cheering noise, like an audience applauding in the distance. Jess would never, ever hear a real audience applauding at this rate. When did she ever have time to write and polish hilarious stand-up material? She was always, *always* chained to the kitchen sink, performing dreary chores from hours before dawn to long after midnight.

She poured milk from the tiresome bottle into Granny's favourite tiresome jug – 'Milk must always be served in a jug, dear, never in the bottle! My mother would turn in her grave if she knew there was a milk bottle on the table!' *But what could possibly happen if you did serve milk straight from the bottle? seethed Jess. Would there be a flash of terrible light and a smell of gunpowder, and would Satan himself appear in the kitchen, beaming and claiming us for his own? I don't think so.*

Jess briefly wished that Satan would appear in the kitchen. Anything to distract her from this drudgery. Now she had to find a tray and she just knew the tray would be covered with dried-on bits of egg and smears of tomato sauce. Yes! Here was the Royal Wedding Tray. And yes! There was a smear of dried tomato sauce right across Will's knees. Jess wiped it off with a dishcloth that smelled of death, pigs' breath and old men's pyjamas. Why couldn't somebody keep the dishcloths fragrant? That should have been another job for Woebegone. The wiping had been a disastrous mistake, as it was now the Royal Wedding Tray that smelled of death, pigs' breath and old men's pyjamas. Jess picked up the stinking dishcloth and hurled it, hard, across the room. It came to rest on the radiator under the window. If she left it there, soon the whole kitchen would smell absolutely vile. She left it there.

Now she would have to wash the tray properly, in the sink, under the tap, with washing-up liquid and a new sponge and everything. She looked in the cupboard under the sink. There were no new sponges. Typical! Instead of making sure there were new sponges (nothing could be more important, surely!), her stupid mother spent every moment of her spare time campaigning against war. It was so futile. There would always be war. It was what men did, according to her mum. (Except Dad – he was different.)

Jess was tempted, for a moment, to rip off her own tights and wash the Royal Wedding Tray with them. But it seemed disrespectful. Jess washed the tray with her bare hands, picking off the dried sauce with her nails, and dried it with a piece of kitchen roll. Then she placed a heatproof mat on it for the teapot, then Granny's favourite jug – which, incidentally, was painted with a scene of cows in a field, on which, Jess couldn't help noticing, there wasn't a single cowpat.

Granny was living in a fool's paradise. The woman hadn't a clue.

Oh no! Jess remembered with a gloomy sigh that Granny didn't like tea from a mug. She had her own china cup and saucer. Making this tea had already taken a thousand years. Jess now had to find Granny's cup and saucer, which weren't in their usual place in the china cupboard.

The dishwasher? Jess knew Granny's cup and saucer shouldn't really be put in the dishwasher, but some spiteful person – the same person who inserted the stink into the dishcloth, presumably – might have put them in there.

Jess opened the dishwasher and peered into it. It was like looking into the rancid mouth of hell. It smelled of old pigs' pyjamas and the breath of dead men. Granny's cup and saucer weren't there.

Jess then commenced a search for Granny's sacred cup and saucer, which started with all the kitchen cupboards, then progressed to the ceiling, the floor, the whole of mainland Europe, the face of the moon and the entire solar system, except for the planet Saturn.

Jess stomped back to Granny's room, but with a ferociously controlled stomp because she didn't actually want to get angry with Granny: this fury was all for her own benefit. It was wonderful, in a way, feeling this mad. It gave her a kind of hellish energy. She could have scrubbed the roof, she felt so full of hideous rage. She could have scrubbed every roof in town!

Granny was watching an archaeology programme. She looked up with a fascinated smile. 'They've found the skeleton of a man in Wiltshire,' she reported with angsty satisfaction. 'He was murdered three thousand years ago!'

'So an arrest's not all that likely, then,' observed Jess. 'Granny, where are your special cup and saucer?'

Granny pursed her lips and thought for a moment.

Jess waited, her blood boiling invisibly behind her smile.

'Now where did I have my last cuppa?' mused Granny. 'I know! I was in the sitting room earlier, watching your telly.'

'What a lifestyle you have, Granny!' observed Jess ironically. 'Moving from TV to TV as the mood takes you.'

'This one hurts my eyes sometimes,' said Granny, with a half-complaining sigh that made Jess feel ridiculously guilty. It wasn't *her* fault Granny's TV hurt her eyes, but maybe she should just accept the guilt anyway. She already felt guilty about global warming, even though her own contribution to it wasn't more significant than that of anyone else who eats beans sometimes.

Jess went to the sitting room and found Granny's cup and saucer on the coffee table. How could Granny just leave dirty stuff lying around like this? That was supposed to be Jess's job. She was the teenager around here. She'd heard that when people get old they often have a Second Childhood. Well, it seemed that Granny was embarking on a Second Teenagehood. Maybe Granny would soon start shouting at Mum, teetering about on killer heels and staying out late. Jess picked up the cup and saucer, carried them to the kitchen, and washed and dried them. Such heroism is rarely seen nowadays.

Finally the tea tray was ready, and Jess carried it ceremoniously to Granny's room.

Granny looked up brightly and clapped her little paws. 'Oooh, lovely, dear! You're an absolute angel!' she cried.

If only she knew. Jess could already feel the horns sprouting from her brow, and her feet were beginning to get that hoofish feeling so popular in the blackest pits of hell.

At this point – luckily, perhaps – the doorbell rang.

'I expect Mum's lost her key again,' remarked Granny acidly from her sea of tapestry.

Jess mooched moodily to the door, pausing for a split second by the hall mirror to check that she did indeed look her absolute worst.

Yes, there she was: spots, hair so greasy a fried egg might recently have adorned it, a nose which seemed to become more shapeless every day, a forehead dotted with blackheads, and eyelids with mascara which had seeped into every little crease. All this beauty was crowned with the kind of scowl not usually available outside high-security prisons.

She slouched to the door and flung it open.

It was Fred.

Chapter 3

Jess couldn't hide her shock and horror. Her heart came hurtling out of her mouth and bounced off down the front path. Her stomach turned a somersault. Her knees knocked audibly. She made an attempt to prise the scowl off her face and replace it with something less aggressive, more stylish and offhand. However, she could tell that her facial expression wasn't working. The stylish, offhand look felt slightly too small for her face. She couldn't quite cram all her features into it. Her lips started twitching.

Fred, on the other hand, looked completely relaxed and normal. 'Hi,' he said, as if he always did this. As if he'd knocked on her door every day for the past few weeks since he'd been going out with Jodie.

Wait! Maybe Fred and Jodie had split up! Maybe he'd come round to prostrate himself before Jess and beg her forgiveness? Jess had feverishly rehearsed the fantasy a thousand times. Fred would stare torment-edly at her, his eyes wild, his clothes kind of neglected (but not smelly) and he would rave on and on about how unworthy he was to even kiss the pavements she walked on. He would promise never to look at another girl for the rest of his life if only she'd take him back. And if she wouldn't, he'd live in her front garden under the hedge and moan tragically every time she walked past.

'Have you got a French dictionary I could borrow?' he asked calmly, as if talking to somebody he'd met once at a very underwhelming party. 'I've lost mine.'

'Oh yeah!' said Jess casually, as if she could hardly remember who he was and couldn't be bothered to try. 'Come in for a minute.'

Oh why had she said that – 'for a minute' – when really she wanted Fred to come in for a lifetime?

'Come up to my room,' said Jess, trying not to make it sound romantic.

Fred followed her in silence.

As they neared the bottom of the stairs, Granny called out, 'Who is it?'

'Only Fred,' answered Jess, trying to force a kind of nonchalant light-heartedness into her voice, which came out like a strangled wail. Granny must not, absolutely must not, say anything inappropriate right now.

'Oh, how lovely!' cried Granny. 'Fred, come here and let me look at you!'

Jess and Fred exchanged the briefest of glances.

'I get this all the time,' murmured Fred. 'Mostly from women over sixty – they seem to want to knit jumpers for me.' He went into Granny's room and awkwardly smiled down at her.

'Fred, dear!' beamed Granny, holding up her hands. 'How lovely to see you!'

Fred wasn't at his best talking to grown-ups. Realising that some kind of physical greeting was unavoidable, he hesitated, then grabbed one of her paws, shook it in the way one shakes a salt cellar and dropped it.

'Hi, Mrs – er,' he replied. Oh no! He'd forgotten her name. 'Jordan.' He hazarded a guess.

'I'm not Mrs Jordan, Fred!' said Granny. 'Jordan is Jess's father's name. I'm Jess's mother's mother.'

'I do know that, of course,' said Fred, looking about as comfortable as a man who suspects a rat may have entered his trousers. 'Sorry. I'm a nincompoop.'

'Interestingly, though,' Granny droned on (whenever she began a sentence with *interestingly*, somehow it ended up being appallingly dull), 'and coincidentally, my surname is a river, too. Like the River Jordan.'

'Let me guess,' said Fred. 'Mrs . . . Nile? Mrs Mississippi? Mrs Yangtze? Mrs Amazon? Mrs . . . Euphrates?'

Jess was impressed by Fred's river savvy. If only she'd known how extensive his river knowledge was, she'd never have dumped him but would instead have made plans to navigate up the Amazon every Friday after school. 'I didn't know you were so into rivers,' she remarked.

'There's a lot about me you don't know,' said Fred. This comment sounded dark, sinister and slightly aggressive. Jess wished he hadn't said it. Fred himself looked as if he wished he hadn't said it – but then he looked like that every time he opened his mouth. He was always flinching and cringing and frowning at his own remarks.

'It's Brooke!' said Granny with a triumphant air.

'Your name?' asked Fred, managing to sound impressed by Granny's staggeringly boring revelation.

'I prefer Euphrates.' Jess tried to jolly things along. 'Or Mississippi. That would be the best. Missus Mississippi.'

'So you're Mrs Brooke?' Fred seemed to be trying to fix Granny's name in his head.

'No,' said Granny. 'Brooke was my maiden name. My married name is Ramsbottom, but I don't like it so much because it has an unfortunate ring to it.'

Jess sighed. She was beginning to feel that Granny had cast a spell on them and they'd now have to spend the next three thousand years talking to her about names and rivers. 'Well, Granny . . .' Jess hinted heavily.

'Yes, yes! Off you go, then!' Granny beamed as if she imagined they were longing to throw themselves into each other's arms, which was, of course, sadly not the case. 'And, Fred, you can just call me Granny,' she said with a kindly smile. 'You're almost family, after all.' And she performed an atrocious wink.

Jess was mortified. Though she loved Granny dearly, she was quite tempted, at this point, to seize her Elvis tapestry, rip it to shreds and stuff the shreds up Granny's nostrils. Almost family! What on earth was she implying?

'Ah, well,' said Jess, heroically stifling her fury. 'Got to lend Fred a dictionary.'

She turned and ran lightly upstairs. Fred followed and Jess hoped she wasn't leaving a waft of sweaty air behind her. She had a feeling she'd been wearing these tights for two days. Still, it was too late to worry about that. Fred was here – right here! For the first time in weeks! OK, he'd only come for a dictionary . . . but had he? Or was it just an excuse?

Pausing outside her bedroom door for a moment, she looked back playfully and whispered, 'Sorry, Granny's getting a bit eccentric.'

'Oh no,' replied Fred politely. 'She's a legend.'

Jess opened her bedroom door and plunged resolutely into the chaos within. Agh! Smiling down from the bulletin board was her hideous cartoon of Jodie and Fred getting married!

Chapter 4

With a single bound Jess tore the cartoon down off the board and stuffed it under her duvet.

'What was that?' enquired Fred. 'Something you didn't want me to see? What could that be?' His eyes were dancing and he looked just like he used to in the good old days. To him this was evidently a huge joke.

'Nothing!' Jess cried. Fred was grinning. This was the worst moment of her life so far. Fred must never ever see the cartoon. She would literally rather drop dead on the spot. Although Jess had a horrible suspicion that, if she were to collapse unconscious at his feet, Fred would take a peek at the mysterious piece of paper stashed away under the duvet *before* calling an ambulance. 'It's just my weight loss chart!' lied Jess hastily.

'What weight loss?' Fred was only teasing, but it

hurt. Jess knew she was porkier than ever and it was cruel of him to hint as much.

'My rather tragic eating probs are private, Fred Parsons!' Jess tried to sound buoyant and good-humoured, but her voice quivered and cracked.

Fred gave her a sceptical look. 'Oh yeah?' he drawled in a mocking tone. 'Eating probs? I don't think so. I think that paper's something much more interesting.'

'It's not!' Jess was aware she sounded like a spoilt child. 'But even if it was, it's private! You can't just come in here and demand to see my private stuff!'

Fred looked round the room at the piles of dirty clothes on the floor, the scribbles and doodles on her desk, the open books, the Post-it notes, her teddy bear Rasputin cuddling up to an old Barbie doll.

'There's no need to see anything,' he said, still with a taunting glint in his eye. 'It's pretty much all in yer face.'

'But I didn't know you were coming!'

'But you invited me up!' Fred's eyes were still twinkling. He just didn't seem to have realised that Jess was really, really upset about the situation.

'So it's a French–English dictionary you need, is it?' asked Jess crisply. She had to distract him from the wretched cartoon.

Fred hesitated, his eyes dancing. 'Never mind the dictionary for a moment,' he said. 'Let's just take a peek at this massive secret.' And suddenly he grabbed the edge of the duvet.

Before he could whip it up, Jess barged into him, knocking him on to the bed. The paper crackled beneath them as they wrestled. Jess tried to grab Fred's wrists, but even though he always described himself as puny and feeble, he was stronger than she was and slipped out of her grasp. He wriggled away and headed for the edge of the duvet again. Jess threw herself on top of him. She had to stop him! She kind of butted him off the bed and he flew forward, hitting his face on the corner of her desk. There was a loud and quite horrible crack. Jess felt sick.

Fred stayed motionless for a moment, half-kneeling on the floor with his back to her. Jess was terrified he would keel over. She had killed Fred! He gasped a couple of times, however, and raised his hand to his cheekbone. Then he clambered to his feet clumsily, with his back still turned to her, and stood holding his face for a moment.

'Fred!' she stammered. 'Are – are you OK?'

He didn't reply immediately, just uttered a few more stifled curses and groans of pain.

'Fred!' She scrambled off the bed and went round to look at his face. His right cheekbone was really red, but there wasn't any blood. 'Are you OK?'

'Stop asking if I'm OK,' he snapped. 'Of course I'm not OK. I come round to borrow a dictionary and I get beaten up.'

'Listen, Fred!' Though concerned about his injury, Jess was still indignant – at least, she was indignant if he wasn't seriously hurt. 'You tried to see some of my secret stuff! Even though I told you it was private, you insisted! That's way out of order! And then you tried to get what you wanted by force, so of course I fought back!'

'Girls! Supposed to be the weaker sex!' grumbled Fred. 'Honestly, you fight like savages.'

'I did not fight like a savage!' shouted Jess. 'I just pushed you off the bed!'

'I expect I've cracked my skull,' said Fred gloomily. 'I'd better go.' He headed for the door.

'Wait! Don't you want the dictionary?'

'No.' He was heading for deep self-pity now, though, being Fred, he couldn't resist a touch of self-parody, too. 'I don't suppose I'll ever do French again. I've probably got a brain injury. I'll probably collapse on the way home and be trampled to death by penguins.'

'Penguins?' asked Jess, puzzled. 'Why penguins?'

'Why not penguins?' Fred shrugged. 'I admit it's an odd thought. It must be a sign of brain damage. If you do find any bits of brain on the carpet, just shove them in the fridge and you can always clone me after I've gone.'

'Don't flatter yourself,' sneered Jess. 'I'd rather clone the school caretaker.' (The caretaker was famous for his repulsive appearance and strange gassy smell.)

Fred walked gingerly to the door, opened it and stood there for a moment. 'See you,' he said. 'Unless my vision goes, that is. If it does, you'll have to pass me notes in Braille.'

Jess was really worried about him but also still furious at his behaviour. 'Goodbye,' she said haughtily. 'I assume you can show yourself out. That is, if your brain's still working.' And she shut the door in his face.

She stood there in her room with her heart hammering in distress. She heard his footsteps going down the stairs and through the hall. She heard some faint cry from Granny, presumably some kind of goodbye, which he ignored. She heard him open the front door and let himself out. And she heard the door slam behind him with a hollow, final sound.

Jess was stunned. She couldn't believe what had just happened. It must count as the worst five minutes ever. Was Fred really so desperate for that dictionary? If so, why hadn't he taken it with him? Or had he just used that as an excuse to see her? Why hadn't she remembered the *You may kick the bride!* cartoon was stuck up on her noticeboard? She could have left him waiting downstairs with Granny just for half a minute while she 'tidied her room'. If only she'd done that, Fred could still be right here with her – and who knows what delicious things might have happened: apologies, reconciliation, hugs . . .

But it wasn't all her fault. Why hadn't Fred respected her privacy? Why had he been determined to spy on her hidden document? And why had he turned it into a stupid fight, for goodness' sake? It was all so utterly insane.

And the fight itself had been so horrible. In the past, when Jess and Fred had been an item, fights had been fun, tickly, giggly events. But this fight had been desperate and awful, and it had ended up with someone really being hurt. Jess felt her stomach lurch with anxiety at the possibility that Fred might have actually cracked his skull. She shouldn't have let him walk home! Maybe she should have called an ambulance!

No, it was stupid to think like that, Jess told herself firmly. It was just an unfortunate accident. Fred shouldn't have been so nosy and Jess had a right to privacy.

Jess sighed wearily. Fred may have gone off with a sore head, but she felt sore herself, right through to her very heart and soul. She flipped over the duvet cover and got out her cartoon. She regretted ever drawing it and couldn't bear the sight of the thing. She screwed the cartoon up into a ball, went to the bathroom and flushed it down the lavatory. It took three flushes before it finally disappeared. Then Jess went back into her room, lay down on the bed and stared at the wall.

Chapter 5

The next morning, Jess walked to school with Flora. She'd decided not to mention anything about Fred's visit last night. It was the kind of embarrassing event she wanted to totally forget. And though Jess adored Flora, she wasn't completely sure she could trust her not to mention it to anybody else.

Sunshine was bouncing off Flora's new zebra-print nails which displayed her passion for Africa. The air snaked warmly round their necks; they might almost have been on safari.

'Isn't it amazing!' gushed Flora. 'Spring's really here – you can feel it in the air. Are you wearing sunscreen?'

'Of course!' lied Jess. Another reason not to be cheerful. Flora had been nagging her all year to wear sunscreen and she'd only remembered twice. By now she'd probably destroyed the top layer of her skin, and by the age of twenty-five her face would look like the moon, complete with craters and crashed spaceships.

'What shall we do at the weekend?' mused Flora.

'Let's get out of this dump,' snapped Jess. She was slightly surprised to hear herself say that. When she'd got up this morning, she'd resolved to put the fight with Fred right out of her mind, to pretend it had never happened, so nobody need ever know. Unless, of course, Fred had been telling people about it. 'Let's go somewhere new, somewhere we've never been before. Let's visit the homeless.' Jess had to stop being bitter and become delightful, generous and, if possible, blonde. 'We could hug the homeless,' she went on recklessly. 'I even know where some homeless people live – under the railway bridge.'

Flora looked startled. Though she was used to Jess's unexpected off-the-wall ideas, this one was a humdinger. 'Would the homeless want us to hug them, though?' asked Flora anxiously.

'I'm going to hug the homeless whether they like it or not,' announced Jess ominously. 'And then I'm going to go down to the dog pound and hug all the unwanted dogs.'

'Jess, those dogs can be kind of dangerous. They

can bite. And anyway, if you hug them you'll cruelly raise their hopes, and they'll think you're going to adopt them. You couldn't adopt them all!'

'Let's be honest, I couldn't adopt a single one of them,' admitted Jess. 'The only fluffy thing allowed in our house is Granny. In fact, she's the nearest thing I've got to a pet. I took her for a walk in the park last Sunday and threw sticks for her.'

'Oh, come on, Jess,' persisted Flora. 'What shall we do this weekend *really*?'

'I won't be allowed to do anything,' said Jess grimly. She was still thinking about how much she longed for a dog, and how resolutely her mum always said no. 'I think my mum was a torturer in a previous existence. I feel sorry for the people who lose their library books.' Her mum was the local librarian and Jess assumed that her attitude to library users was the same as her attitude to Jess. She imagined her mum walking up and down the bookshelves and giving the evil eye to anybody who even dared to cough.

Even as she said the word *torturer*, Jess felt the tiniest frisson of guilt. Her parents weren't too bad, to be honest. They stayed out of trouble, they never rowed and, though they'd got divorced years ago, they'd become good friends. Jess hoped nobody was eavesdropping on this conversation from heaven. Some people believed that St Peter wrote down all the details of everybody's behaviour in a big thick book, and when you got to the Pearly Gates he'd interrogate you about your crimes and sins.

Please, Pete, whispered Jess secretly, in the back of her mind. *When I called my mum a former torturer I didn't really mean it. I'm grateful for the terrific job she's done, bringing me up and stuff. Apart from the cabbage soup.*

'If only your dad still lived in St Ives,' sighed Flora, 'we could go down there and visit him.'

Dad's stylish seaside lifestyle in romantic, faraway St Ives had come to an end and he now lived less than half a mile away, in a tiny flat overlooking a hideous car park behind the dental surgery. At least it was only ten minutes' walk from Jess's house instead of two hundred miles. Jess was tempted to defend her dad, even though she herself had been really annoyed when he announced that he and his long-term boyfriend Phil were separating. Apparently it was Phil's money which had been funding their glamorous life in the fabulous white house by the sea.

It wasn't Flora's job to be annoyed about any of that stuff. Flora's own dad was, after all, a total ogre and it was only the thought of St Peter peering down, with pen poised, that made Jess bite her lip and refrain from launching into a dad-dissing extravaganza.

'Maybe we could go to St Ives anyway, at half-term,' Jess suggested, 'and stay in a hostel or something. That would be cool. Although of course I have no money.'

Flora had been slaving away in a small supermarket every Thursday evening since the dawn of time – or for about six weeks, anyway – and Jess knew she had accumulated a nice little stash of money, even though she was on the minimum wage. Jess herself had been meaning to apply for some kind of job but had only managed a bit of babysitting. Her dad had paid her for helping him to move into his little flat but, being a starving artist, he wasn't exactly loaded, and Jess had felt bad about taking any money from him at all. She'd even insisted on giving him ten pounds back of the fifteen he'd paid her. She hoped St Peter had been watching at that moment but, knowing her recent luck, St Peter had probably been having a coffee break.

Of course Jess and Fred had always planned to create a comedy routine which was meant to make them fabulously rich and famous – eventually. They'd even done one or two performances for little kids when their friends had been babysitting. But they'd never had the cheek – or the guts – to ask for a fee, and besides, since Fred and Jodie had got together, somehow Jess and Fred's comedy partnership had shrivelled away into nothing. And Jess had let it shrivel, because she'd felt kind of paralysed when Jodie grabbed Fred, as if, now Jess wasn't Fred's girlfriend any more, she didn't have a right even to be his buddy, like she had been for years, before they'd ever become an item.

'Wouldn't it be kind of sad going to St Ives now your dad isn't there?' asked Flora tentatively.

'Yeah, you're right,' Jess agreed.

St Ives would also be full of memories of Fred, since he'd secretly come down to see her there last summer, and the surprise of seeing him waiting by the harbour had been the very best moment of her life so far. That image – of him standing leaning against the sea wall, grinning, with the sea sparkling behind him – was burned into Jess's memory. It was the screen saver of her brain, and her mind returned to it again and again in moments of sadness.

'I want to go somewhere completely, totally new,' said Jess, resolutely closing down the Fred-in-St-Ives image.

They had reached the school gates, a location that was all too familiar.

'Hey, Jordan! Barclay!' Jess and Flora were being hailed by Mackenzie, who had started to use surnames for everybody. Mackenzie had had a growth spurt recently and could now look the girls in the eye without having to use a periscope. 'Listen up!' he said urgently. 'We've had the best idea for what to do this weekend!'

Ben Jones was standing behind him, hands in pockets. His legendary handsomeness was still like something out of a fairytale; right now he seemed clothed in golden light, a bit like an angel, because the sun was behind him, whereas Jess had the sun's dazzling beams in her face and was squinting at him like some kind of wizened turnip. Although she had got over her crush on Ben Jones long ago, she still wanted to look as fabulous as possible whenever he was around.

What brilliant idea for relentless weekend fun had Mackenzie and Ben Jones come up with? Jess hoped it was going to be good. Unfortunately Mackenzie's ideas were often utter trash, so the chances were, at best, fifty–fifty.

Chapter 6

'My cousin Adam, right?' Mackenzie launched into one of his announcements. He had a picturesque collection of cousins, many of whom were in some way slightly weird. 'He's got this mate who's well rich, right? His dad is, like, an old rock star, and they've got this amazing huge mansion-type place out in the country, and his parents have also got a beach house in St Barts that cost three million or something. Anyway, his parents are away at the moment, so he's organising this amazing house party at the country place. It's gonna be massive! We've all gotta go!'

'Cool!' enthused Flora. She'd always had a soft spot for Mackenzie, even when he had been microscopic.

Jess had a sinking feeling. No way was she ever going to be allowed to go to a house party. Mum would say no. Dad would say no. Granny would say no. Even her teddy bear Rasputin would say no. 'Where exactly is it?' she asked, turning for a moment into her mother.

'Uh – down, uh, near . . . Not sure actually. Down in, like, Devon or somewhere,' said Mackenzie.

Jess knew where Devon was as she'd often had to travel through it in order to get to Cornwall to visit her dad, back in the good old days. 'Devon's a bit far away, though,' she commented.

'Nah, it's no problem!' insisted Mackenzie. 'There are trains, buses – you name it. Or we could hitch.'

Jess's heart sank another seven miles at the thought of hitching, something her mum had absolutely forbidden under all circumstances. Jess had been forced to make a promise Never To Hitch and sign it in blood. 'Yeah, right.' She shrugged. 'We'd get picked up by a serial killer who, like, chops us into little pieces and puts us into a pie.'

'The bus,' Ben drawled from beneath his dazzling halo of sunlight, 'is, er, takes three and a half hours, and if you have a Young Person's Coachcard you get a, um, reduction on the fare.' Jess had often noticed that, although Ben Jones's appearance was golden, his conversational style was one hundred per cent wooden.

It did not detract from his wonderfulness, however –
in fact, his hesitant shy way of talking only made him
more endearing. And it was refreshing to know that
you didn't have to listen with your whole brain. Just
half would do.

'How much is the fare?' asked Flora, sensing an
opportunity for her beloved maths. 'And how much is
the Young Person's Coachcard?'

Nobody knew.

'Hey, never mind about that!' Mackenzie went on.
'Listen! They're going to have a band called Bleeding
Entrails, and a hog roast. This place has got, like,
turrets and stuff, and about thirty bedrooms, and you
can get out on the roof and there's even, like, some old
dungeon left over from the fourteenth century or
something.'

Flora looked thoughtful. 'My dad would never let
me go.' She sighed. 'It does sound really amazing, but
he would just never agree to it.'

Jess knew her own mum would be similarly nega-
tive. In certain moods her mum wouldn't let her go
anywhere by any means of transport whatsoever. In
Mum's raging imagination, even walking had its
perils. Sometimes Jess thought her mum would never
really relax unless she'd managed to tie Jess to the

sofa and burn all her shoes so she couldn't leave the house.

'No need for the parents to know, baby!' Mackenzie ranted on.

Jess thought it was rather lame for Mackenzie to call Flora 'baby', but Flora looked as if she quite liked it and even pretended to scratch the side of her face to display her magnificent zebra nails.

'Tell 'em you're staying with Jess!' blagged Mackenzie, his black curls vibrating with energy.

'Oh yeah?' remarked Jess scornfully. 'And what do I tell my mum? That I'm going to Flora's?'

'Exactamundo!' beamed Mackenzie.

'We've tried that so many times, you idiot!' Jess shook her head in disbelief. 'Mum would just inevitably phone Flora's mum to check up on me before I'd got halfway down the front path.'

It was annoying that Mackenzie was so obsessed by this house party idea. She was distracted, however, by the sight of Jodie and Fred approaching – wearing masks. (Fred's mask was a gorilla, Jodie's a zombie.) Jess prepared to have her heartstrings ripped to shreds for the first time that day.

Jodie's zombie mask was hideous. Both cheeks had stitched wounds and the teeth were yellow and snaggy.

Huge warts on the chin and bristly eyebrows completed the ensemble.

'Jodie!' cried Jess. 'You've had a facelift! You look amazing!'

'You should get one, too, Jess!' replied the zombie, laughing. One of the annoying things about the Fred and Jodie Situation was that Jodie wasn't completely awful. OK, she was kind of loud and pushy, but she was basically a kind-hearted person. It would have been so much easier if Jess had been able to hate her. But now Jess was taking Granny's advice and trying to be marvellous, she was going to be wonderfully kind to her, no matter what.

'Great masks!' enthused Mackenzie. 'Where did you get them?'

'Just the joke shop!' boomed Jodie. 'Fred gets a special price because basically he *is* a joke!'

Jess only gave Fred's mask the briefest glance. There was something unsettling about seeing the gleam of his eyes in the holes in the gorilla face. This was the first time she'd seen him since their fight in her bedroom. She still felt sick about that – sick and guilty. What if Fred was wearing a mask to hide the terrible injury she'd inflicted on him during their fight?

'Why masks, though?' asked Flora.

'It's to get us in the mood for the half-marathon!' explained Jodie. 'We might wear masks to help raise extra money for charity. Ugh! This thing's really itchy, though!' She ripped off the mask and rubbed her cheeks energetically. Jess noticed that Jodie didn't have any spots right now – in fact, she had a positive glow. At one time she'd been the Queen of Zits.

'Why a zombie?' asked Jess.

'We might change our minds,' said Jodie. 'This is just, like, our current plan.'

Jess felt a wave of jealousy. Jodie had persuaded Fred to ditch the habits of a lifetime by putting on trainers and running for charity. Jess had never even managed to get Fred up off his sofa. 'When is the half-marathon again?' she asked. 'I'll be there at the finishing line, waiting for you with a roll of tin foil. And then I'm going to roast the pair of you in a hot oven, with a lemon and thyme stuffing.'

Jodie shrieked with hysterical laughter. She always cracked up at Jess's jokes. She had never gone all jealous and scratchy with Jess, even though it would have been easy to fall into that trap; after all, Jess was the charismatic ex-girlfriend. *Although I'm about as charismatic as a brown paper bag*, thought Jess with marvellous modesty, the sort of modesty which really ought to be on show for everybody to admire – except then it wouldn't be modesty.

Jodie carried on talking about the half-marathon and, though Jess tried to concentrate, she was instead distracted by the ridiculous pantomime of Fred trying to take his mask off and getting the elastic caught on his ears, then pulling it crossly and being hit in the face by it. Jess was aware all this was happening, but she didn't look directly at him. She wanted him to think she was ignoring him.

Fred would just *have* to be a professional comedian because nobody would ever take him seriously in a proper job. She could sense, out of the corner of her eye, that he'd got his mask off now, but was he looking at her? Jess was desperate to know, but she didn't dare to steal even a tiny glance, because nothing would be worse than to look at Fred and find that he was looking at Jodie with an expression of foolish adoration, for example. But if he was, so what? Now Jess was determined to be marvellous, surely she wanted them to be happy. Jess smiled marvellously at Jodie through gritted teeth.

'Hey, man, what happened to your face?' yelled Mackenzie excitedly. 'Did Jodie beat you up for being an idiot?'

'Ouch!' Ben Jones flinched slightly, like somebody who has seen an accident. 'How did you get that one, Fred?'

'Walked into a door.' Fred shrugged. 'I wasn't paying attention.'

Jess turned to look. He had a huge black eye – well, it was more a mixture of red, purple and blue. She squirmed in horror.

'Oh yeah, the old door excuse?' Mackenzie grinned tauntingly. 'We've all heard that one before. How did you get it really? Who dished it out?'

'Believe me, it was a door,' Fred insisted. 'It's been brewing between us for some time. Me and that door – there have always been bad vibes. Last night, without any provocation at all, it just lashed out. I was texting at the time, so maybe that's why I walked straight into it.'

'Yeah, yeah, pull the other one,' jeered Mackenzie. 'It was Jodie, I can tell – she's got that guilty look.'

'It so was not!' yelled Jodie, thumping Mackenzie roughly on the arm.

'Ow!' shouted Mackenzie. 'Beating me up now, are you? The woman's an animal!' And he backed off theatrically, cradling his arm.

Jodie grinned. She didn't really seem to care that

Mackenzie thought she had given Fred a black eye. For a moment Jess felt absurdly jealous. That was *her* black eye Fred was wearing – not Jodie's. He may not be her boyfriend any more but at least he was still her punchbag. However, she decided to stay silent on the subject. It was all too dodgy and delicate. She didn't even know if Jodie knew that Fred had turned up at her house last night, though why he'd gone round in the first place was still a mystery to Jess.

'Jodie's going to be a bodyguard when she leaves school,' gasped Fred. 'I'm just doing the half-marathon because otherwise she'll beat me up!'

'Shut up, you imbecile!' cried Jodie, slapping him playfully. 'Remember it's for a good cause!' Jodie never seemed to take offence at anything Fred said – everything was just a huge joke. Jess remembered that feeling. When she and Fred had been together, ironical insults and scorn had been their way of showing affection.

'How's His Nibs?' asked Fred, suddenly turning to Jess with a scorching glance.

'Who?' Jess panicked at the suddenness of his look.

'His Nibs, the Nobel Prize Winning Boy Next Door,' Fred went on. 'I assume he's also doing the half-marathon, to add to his CV, which, let's face it, is already six pages long and includes humanitarian work in all seven continents.'

'What, Luke? I haven't seen him for ages.' Jess shrugged, trying to sound marvellously casual. 'He's always going up to Manchester to see his girlfriend.' She stared boldly back at him. Did the expression in Fred's eyes modulate slightly, softening from challenge to relief? Or was it her imagination?

'I thought you and Luke were going to be the Next Big Thing, Jess!' roared Jodie. 'Remember I bet you five quid you'd be snogged by him!'

'Well, I won that bet,' announced Jess with a firm jut of the jaw to conceal the lie, 'so gimme the dough!'

Was it a lie, though? She and Luke had kissed once, but it hadn't been a proper kiss. Their lips had met, as instructed in the manual, but the emptiness of the experience had left her feeling that it was more like some kind of oral t'ai chi or perhaps an unusually close dental check-up. They'd both immediately backpedalled, with Luke apologising and explaining that he'd been trying to forget a girl in Manchester, and Jess acknowledging that she was still not over Fred.

So, for many reasons, Jess had never told anybody about her awkward doomed kiss with Luke. It wasn't just that Jess wanted to win her £5 bet. Above all, she wasn't going to let Fred know she'd snogged Luke. She assumed Fred and Jodie had done a lot of that in the past few weeks, and Jess had tried hard not to torture herself by imagining it – not more than fifteen times a day, anyway. They'd never actually kissed in front of her – they were too considerate to do anything so crass – but Jodie was always playfully kind of mucking about with Fred; pulling his ears, wearing his hoodie, wrestling him to the ground. So far Jess had managed to bear all this without screaming.

Fred had got involved with somebody else, but she hadn't really, and she wanted things to stay like that. She wanted to be loftily indifferent, the ice maiden, the untouchable unattainable goddess. Absolutely marvellous and way out of his league. Or something.

Chapter 7

At lunchtime, in the classroom, the subject of What To Do At The Weekend was resurrected. Mackenzie seemed really determined to go off to the house party in Devon and Ben Jones was half-inclined to go with him. They'd always been virtually inseparable and Fred had predicted that once they left school, Ben would become a major celeb and Mackenzie would be his agent.

'I can't go! I'd really love to, but my dad would kill me,' sighed Flora, admiring her zebra nails and sprawling on a table top.

'I can't, either,' added Jess. 'I can't afford it anyway.'

'Hey! Why don't we have a house party of our own?' yelled Jodie. 'All we need is a house, right?'

'Great idea!' Flora sat up and started to look interested. She sensed an outing for her black-and-white nails. 'But where? It can't be at mine because my dad would go berserk if I even mentioned the idea.'

'It can't be at mine,' warned Jodie, 'because we've only just had the winter barbecue and my mum said I can't have another party for ten years.'

'My mum,' confessed Fred, 'would want to join in. And I'm afraid I'd have psychological problems for the rest of my life.'

'You will anyway, you weirdo!' grinned Jodie. Then she turned to Jess. 'Looks like it's your turn, then, Jess.'

'What, with my mum and granny eavesdropping all night?' Jess shook her head. 'No chance! Fred's mum may want to join in but my family would want to organise it. If you're all coming round to mine it would be for chocolate muffins and pass the parcel.'

'Hmmm,' murmured Fred. 'That sounds strangely attractive . . .'

'Hey!' Mackenzie suddenly remembered something. 'There's that match tonight! You guys have all got to come and support Ben against St Benedict's!'

Ben Jones was the school football captain and tonight they were playing St B's.

'Hey!' exclaimed Jess. 'That's where Luke's dad teaches. He's really, really nice.'

'Well, come to the match, then,' suggested Ben shyly. 'If you, erm, if you're not doing anything else. It's at their ground up beyond the industrial estate.'

'Let's all go!' cried Jodie. 'Support for Ben Jones! Respect!'

Almost immediately the lunch hour was over and it was back to the treadmill of lessons, with no real opportunities for being marvellous. There was, however, the slightly intriguing prospect of watching a football match after school, so Jess fired off a text to her mum warning her she'd be back late.

Instead of the usual brusque-but-adoring response from her busy librarian mother, Jess received the following text: GREAT-AUNT JANE HAS HAD A STROKE AND I'VE GOT TO DRIVE GRANNY UP TO BIRMINGHAM TO SEE HER. WE'LL BE LEAVING TONIGHT AND COMING BACK ON SUNDAY. YOU CAN STAY WITH DAD – IT'S ALL ARRANGED. X

Jess hadn't actually seen Great-Aunt Jane since she was about five, so the news, though sad, was not personally devastating. She was Granny's sister-in-law, and Granny and Jane had always had a rather scratchy relationship. There had been a bit of an emotional tussle over Grandpa, as Jane had never married and idolised her brother. Recently there had been an unseemly row about where to scatter his ashes and who was entitled to do it. Granny had won, with a mixture of native cunning and determination, and had scattered the ashes from a boat in St Ives Bay on a trip down to see Dad and the stylish and wonderful Phil.

'Guess what, guys?' announced Jess, without even pausing to think about the details. 'Looks like I'll be home alone tomorrow night, after all. Mum and Granny are off on a mercy dash.'

'Result!' yelled Jodie, punching the air.

After school, it was a long hard slog across town to St Benedict's sports field, and a fierce wind was blowing. Ben Jones had gone ahead in the team bus, but the rest of the gang had to walk. They passed the Dolphin Cafe, which smelled divinely of cheese pasties, and Jess wished for a split second that instead of spending the next hour or two yelling on a muddy field, she had made the more sensible decision to demolish patisserie with Flora. But it was too late now because dear Ben Jones would be depending on them and such a good-looking and sweet-natured guy deserved support.

The wind was so strong in the town centre that bits of rubbish were being blown about. Jess was just wondering if the gale was rumpling her hair picturesquely, giving her that Cathy-from-*Wuthering-Heights* look that was so eternally chic, when a huge and painful speck of dust, about the size of a grand piano, blew into her right eye.

'Argh!' she gasped.

Instantly her eyelid started a mad twitching and floods of tears coursed down her right cheek. It's bad enough weeping bucketloads from both eyes, but at least that would have been symmetrical. A black river of mascara from one eye was, Jess knew, the ultimate in anti-chic. The terrible eyelid-twitching didn't do her any favours, either; she knew she must look like a crazed poisoner in an early film noir movie.

'My eye! My eye!' she roared, standing stock-still outside the town hall. Her friends gathered round. 'Ouch! Ouch! Ouch! It hurts like mad!'

Instead of being helpful and sympathetic, Fred looked amused – the swine! 'Contact lens on the blink?' he asked with a sardonic smile.

Thank goodness Jess still had one good eye – out of the left one she spotted a ladies' loo. She'd used it before on several occasions to change out of some deeply wrong clothes and into something more low-key – it had been a mistake to combine that leopard-print miniskirt with a flouncy scarlet top.

It was an old-fashioned ladies' room and offered two loos, each with its own porcelain washbasin; they were almost en suites. Jess groped her way into the nearest one and, through floods of tears, locked herself in before turning on the brass taps and washing her eye with handfuls of water. Beyond the gasping and splashing Jess was dimly aware of her friends apparently arguing out in the street.

At last the speck was out of her eye and she inspected the damage. Her left eye was clear and untouched, beautifully mascaraed and stylish. Her right eye was puffy, swollen and bloodshot, with a river of black down her cheek. She looked like someone half-possessed by the devil. Hastily she ransacked her school bag for some make-up.

'Jess?' It was Flora's voice, outside the door. 'Are you still in there? Hurry up!'

'Just a minute! Just a minute!' Panicking, Jess's trembling fingers scrambled through her bag. She knew in her heart of hearts that the eye make-up remover was back home on the bathroom shelf.

'We've got to go NOW!' Flora sounded annoyed. 'Kick-off is at four thirty and Jodie's promised to photograph the team for Ben Jones's Facebook page!'

'Coming! Coming!' Jess abandoned her search for make-up remover, tore off a handful of loo roll and smeared it with liquid soap. She had to keep this away from her eye, but it was her eye that needed to be cleaned. Gingerly she wiped the lower half of her cheek, then a bit higher . . .

'Jess! Come ON!' screeched Flora.

Jess chucked the tissue down the loo and flushed frantically. Her right eye would have to stay black and smeary for now, but there was a chemist's not far away, where she could buy some make-up remover pads and sort her face out before she got to the St Benedict's football match.

She grabbed her school bag and reached for the bolt. But it came off in her hand, and the door wouldn't open. It was jammed shut.

'Jess! Come on!' called Flora hysterically. 'We're gonna be late!'

'The door's jammed!' yelled Jess in desperation. 'The handle thing's come off! I'm locked in!' She rattled the door and tried to prise her fingers round the edge of the bolt, but she couldn't get inside the mechanism.

'Push it! Push it!' yelled Jess.

Flora heaved, but in vain.

'Didn't you see the notice saying this loo is out of order?' shouted Flora.

Jess felt irritated. She had blundered in here, blinded by floods of tears, and now she was stuck. Locked in the loo! How marvellous was that?

'Look,' called Jess, 'tell Jodie and Fred to go on ahead.'

'OK, OK, good idea,' said Flora.

'I can't believe this!' howled Jess. 'Find somebody to get me out of here!'

'Yes, I'll try to get help!' Flora assured her.

Jess leaned her head wearily against the mirror and waited. Luckily Flora was here to help.

Jess looked up and wondered if she could climb out of the cubicle, but because it was one of those old-fashioned loos there was no gap at the top – the walls went right up to the ceiling. She was trapped! The tiny frosted window was strongly defended by iron bars on the outside so it didn't offer an escape route, either. Jess was so tempted to give way to a hysterical attack of claustrophobia and collapse in a shrieking heap. Never had a screaming fit seemed more appropriate. Instead she decided to hold on to her sanity. Here was a chance to be marvellous. People would say, *'Did you hear about Jess Jordan? She was locked in a lavatory and it was a dreadful experience, but she was so marvellous about it! How the town cheered when she finally got out!'*

But maybe she'd never make it out of there! Jess sat down on the loo seat cover and imagined living out the rest of her days in this lavatory. She'd miss out on family life and having children. Her friends and family would club together to buy her one of those very, very thin laptops, which could just about be squeezed under the cubicle door. They'd have to feed her that way, too; thin-crust pizzas would be her daily fare. She would spend her whole life surfing the web and eating pizza. Luckily DVDs were also very thin. To be honest, sacrificing a husband and family was a small price to pay for what seemed like an increasingly attractive lifestyle. Though draughty, the accommodation was at least en suite.

'Jess!' Evidently Flora was back – hallelujah! 'It's all right. Mr Patel is going to help us get you out!'

'Oh, brilliant! Thank you so much!' called Jess, getting up. She wondered who Mr Patel was, but at this precise moment it seemed a bit rude to ask.

'Stand back now!' cried a male voice – presumably Mr Patel, the hero.

Jess wondered if he was going to charge the door with his shoulder, like in a James Bond movie. She shrank towards the back wall – at least, as far as she could without actually flushing herself down the lavatory (the last-resort escape route, though she'd have to go on a strict eight-week diet first).

Mr Patel started rattling the door about. Jess watched as the locking mechanism jumped and jiggled. She felt her cheeks go red with embarrassment as she imagined a great crowd of curious onlookers gathered outside. Maybe somebody would be filming this on their mobile phone and within seconds her predicament would be posted on YouTube.

After an eternity of metallic jiggling, the door moved on its hinges and finally opened. Jess was disappointed to discover that instead of being a tall, handsome, godlike figure, Mr Patel was small, bald and middle-aged. His face seemed anxious and he was holding a screwdriver thingy. Flora was standing beside him, looking pale and irritated.

'Thank you so much!' gushed Jess.

'There's a notice on the door saying this toilet is out of order,' Mr Patel pointed out rather crossly. 'Didn't you see it?'

'No, sorry. I had a speck in my eye,' explained Jess hurriedly, pointing at her own face in rather a foolish fashion. 'I was totally blinded. Look!'

Mr Patel gazed at her hideously disfigured eye and nodded. Jess was annoyed that her eye looked so obviously ghastly.

'Thank you so much!' Jess repeated. 'I'm really sorry to have bothered you!'

'Why don't they put a padlock on the door to stop people from going in there?' asked Flora.

'You know the council,' said Mr Patel gloomily. 'Nowadays it's budget cuts, isn't it? Do you know how much locksmiths charge?'

Flora had to admit that, despite her terrific brain and straight As in every subject under the sun, locksmiths' fees had so far escaped her.

'Hundreds,' said Mr Patel sternly. For a horrible moment Jess wondered if he was going to ask for payment himself. 'Well, thanks ever so much for rescuing me, Mr Patel!' Jess touched him lightly on the arm, smiling her most energetic, adult-charming smile. 'You're my hero!'

Mr Patel looked unimpressed. He shrugged, rolled his eyes at her and went away.

'Where did you find him?' whispered Jess, intrigued.

'He runs the corner shop,' said Flora. 'I think we're going to have to go in there for ice creams for a few weeks to show our gratitude.'

'It's a tough assignment,' said Jess, 'but we'll just have to bite the bullet!'

As they walked out on to the empty pavement, Jess's heart gave a little leap. Fred was standing there.

'Jodie's gone on ahead,' he said, 'but I thought I'd wait in case they had to call the fire brigade or something. Anything for a laugh. And there was always the chance you might be delightfully humiliated.'

'Well, the night is young,' quipped Jess. 'Watch this space.'

Fred scratched his cheek in an edgy way and looked at the pavement for a moment.

He had waited for her! A strange warm little glow wrapped itself around Jess's heart.

'Also, I didn't want to miss a chance to call the whole football thing off,' Fred explained evasively. 'Too bad they managed to get you out.' He shot a sly glance at Jess. It had the merest, tiniest hint of his old teasing way. 'I was hoping you'd be walled up in there for all eternity.'

'Oh boy, I was so hoping that, too!' countered Jess. 'I was going to spend the rest of my days in there, surfing on my laptop and snacking on extra-thin-crust pizza, which you guys were going to shove under the door.'

'The eye looks great, by the way,' Fred went on, a

faint grin playing around the edges of his mouth. 'I'm touched, but really there was no need for you to get a tribute black eye.'

'Oh, I don't know,' hinted Jess. 'I think it was the least I could do.'

'You're a right pair!' laughed Flora. There was a split second of embarrassment at the notion that Jess and Fred might, in some sense, be a pair after all – even if it was only a tendency to a black eye which they shared. 'Come on – football calls!'

Chapter 8

Jess arrived home after the match – a dreary, goal-less draw – to find Mum and Granny packing their bags.

'We have to drive up tonight,' Mum explained. 'Because of the visiting hours at the hospital, we'd never make the morning session if we drove up tomorrow. Granny wants to see as much as she can of Jane.' Mum dropped her voice confidentially. 'I think there's a lot of unfinished business between them,' she whispered. 'Go and give her a hand – she's feeling a bit fragile.'

Jess went into Granny's room and found her looking at an old photo album. She didn't look fragile – only thoughtful – but she brightened up when Jess came in.

'Hello, dear!' she beamed. 'How's everything?'

'Oh, fine, thanks, Granny,' replied Jess. 'I got locked in a lavatory today, but it was quite enjoyable really.'

'I meant to ask you last night,' said Granny. 'What was all that noise in your room yesterday, when Fred came? I thought he was murdering you for a minute.'

'Hard luck, Granny!' Jess kneeled at Granny's feet and grabbed her funny old hand. 'I know you'd love nothing more than to have a stylish homicide in your very own home so you could do a Miss Marple, but Fred was merely showing me his break-dancing moves.' Jess would have to laugh about this idea in private afterwards – the thought of Fred break-dancing was too hilarious for words.

'Is that break-dancing thing where boys bounce around on their heads?' asked Granny, looking mystified.

'Sort of.' Jess nodded. 'But listen, Granny, I'm so sorry to hear Great-Aunt Jane's ill.'

Granny's expression changed and she looked pensive. She showed Jess the photo album. It was open at a page of little photos of three people at the seaside – two women and a man.

'Here we are, in our bikinis,' mused Granny, stroking the photo in a wistful way. Jess felt sorry for Granny being old and not being able to wear bikinis any more. 'The thing was,' Granny went on, 'Jane never married, and she was very fond of Grandpa. I suppose girls are always fond of their brothers. She was certainly a bit competitive with me. Jane didn't approve of me at all. She thought I was a bad influence, you know, what with the leather miniskirts and the motorbikes and everything.' Granny's past as a rocker had always fascinated Jess.

'But Grandpa was a rocker, too,' Jess remarked proudly.

'Yes, but Jane wasn't. We had quite a few arguments when we were younger. You'd call them "issues" nowadays. I have to go and make my peace with her, I suppose, in case she snuffs it.'

At this point Mum put her head round the door. 'Right, Jess,' she said. 'You'll be staying with Dad, OK?'

Jess's mind clicked into plotting mode. She had made arrangements to spend Saturday night right here in a low-budget but nevertheless enjoyable evening with her best mates. However, she could go to Dad's tonight and soften him up nicely, so he wouldn't insist on her staying for Saturday as well. She quite fancied a father-daughter bonding session anyway.

Jess felt slightly guilty that the last few times he'd invited her to come over for a meal or to go to the movies, she'd not been able to make it. But, then, he surely understood that she had a relentless social diary to maintain. She'd need to deluge him with charm, though, if he was going to abandon his plans for their weekend without getting all moody. Sometimes she thought her dad was quite like a teenage girl himself.

Jess packed an overnight bag, kissed Mum and Granny goodbye, and headed over to Paternal Towers.

She toiled up the rather shabby communal staircase – such a contrast from his former white-walled palace by the sea – and then pressed the horrid buzzer that sounded like a bullfrog in a swamp. Jess pulled a hideous face because she knew he was peering through the security spyhole to make sure she wasn't an evil attacker wielding an axe. Then the door was unbolted – Dad was such a wuss, locking himself in at eight o'clock! And there he stood in all his glory: tall, thin, fair-haired and blue-eyed. Why oh why hadn't she inherited his genes instead of the dark, waddling, muffin-top ones from Mum?

'Daddo!' Jess hurled herself into his arms. 'You Baddo! Fabulous to see you!'

Dad wasn't brilliant at hugs – he really needed six weeks at hug school to transform his efforts from the wooden, stringy cuddle of a hesitant marionette towards something a little more full-blooded. But he did mean well, bless him. Jess hugged him so hard she almost cracked his ribs.

'Jess! You look wonderful!' He was more at home shovelling compliments on her and, as far as Jess was concerned, that was just dandy. She knew perfectly well that her right eye was still bleary from the mascara crisis earlier and that certain parts of her face had taken on a lumpy quality, rather like a cheap duvet, but it was reassuring that somebody still thought she looked wonderful.

'Dad, that's rubbish! But you, on the other hand, look dazzling!' She had to heap compliments on him. What do men worry about? Ah, of course – going bald! 'Your hair's so thick! Are you using a new shampoo or something? And that shirt is my favourite! It brings out the amazing sky-blue of your eyes.'

'Phil gave me this two Christmases ago,' said Dad, looking down at his shirt with a doleful expression.

Whoops! Jess must at all costs steer the conversation away from Dad's much-missed ex, Phil, who, besides being handsome, fun and sporty, had also rather conveniently been rich. Ever since he'd been dumped by Phil, Dad had looked a bit down in the mouth, especially when the name 'Phil' was mentioned

– even when it was just a word, not a name. Once Jess had even felt a twinge of guilt when she'd asked Dad to help her 'phil' in a form.

'Hey, Dad! Your flat looks great! You've moved that bookcase, right?'

'But you've seen that four times before.' Dad looked puzzled.

'Yeah, maybe, but I didn't really appreciate it until now. What's that lovely smell?'

'I had beans on toast earlier,' said Dad.

'Toast!' exclaimed Jess. 'It's only the best smell in the world! They should bottle it and sell it as after-shave! What's for supper?'

'I thought we could have a cheesy omelette,' he said, very obviously pulling himself out of a gloomy moment. 'And tomorrow we could paint the bathroom – you've been nagging me to do that ever since I moved in, and I've decided to let you choose the colour!' Coming from a man who made his living painting – or rather, failed to make his living painting – this was a big deal, even though Dad's normal style was seagulls rather than bathrooms.

Jess had to head off his plans for Saturday evening, when she would be hosting Flora and Fred and the inevitable Jodie. She looked around for something else to talk about. She hadn't softened Dad up nearly enough yet. He'd have to be putty in her hands before she dropped the bombshell about tomorrow night.

'What lovely forks!' she cried, randomly selecting Dad's cutlery – he'd already laid the table for supper.

'Forks?' Dad was understandably puzzled.

'I've just got into knives and forks recently,' said Jess, seizing the fork and racking her brains for something to say about it. 'I think I might fancy being a homeware designer. Maybe I've inherited your fabulous artistic genes.' She gave him a flattering smile, even though her heart wasn't in it and she could feel the sides of the smile twitching slightly, like scaffolding that's about to give way.

'A designer? You?' asked Dad, looking astonished. 'I thought you were destined for a career as a stand-up comedian?'

'Oh, you know . . .' Jess studied the fork. It was stainless steel with four prongs. It was hard to imagine anyone ever bothering to design cutlery. What changes could you make? Three prongs? Five prongs? A pink handle?

'How is Fred?' asked Dad suddenly.

Jess's heart gave a lurch. She felt the tables being

turned so violently she almost had to sit down. Now Dad was the one taking the initiative.

'Is he still going around with that girl with the nose?'

'Yes, he's still seeing Jodie.' Jess tried to be brisk and matter of fact. 'And yes, she still has a nose.'

'For goodness' sake!' cried Dad impatiently. 'Tell the lad to get a grip and come back to where he belongs!'

Jess decided she should sit down. Her legs felt a bit weak. She wasn't getting enough exercise – not like Fred and Jodie, who were running miles on a daily basis. 'Dad, I dumped Fred, remember? And for a good reason.'

'Yes, but he's suffered enough,' Dad argued. 'And, more to the point, so have you. I did wonder about you and that chap next door, though – what's his name? Luke?'

'Luke was never in the picture,' lied Jess. 'We're just friends. And I haven't seen him for ages because every spare moment of his time is spent in Manchester with his Glamorous Girlfriend.'

'Nice chap,' observed Dad thoughtfully, 'but obviously not your type. Fred's the one. I don't need to tell you that – you know it yourself.'

Jess's head slumped into her hands and she stared at

the wall. There was a short pause. 'Look, Dad, can we please not talk about Fred?' she sighed. 'I've got used to the situation and he seems perfectly happy with Jodie.'

'How could anybody be happy with Jodie compared to you?' asked Dad supportively, but somehow also managing to be very irritating indeed.

'You're biased,' said Jess.

'I don't think so,' Dad went on. 'I've hardly spoken to the girl, but Jodie scares the living daylights out of me. She's a bulldozer.'

'Some guys like girls with powerful personalities,' argued Jess. It was weird, trying to persuade her dad that she was fine about Fred and Jodie.

'Well, good luck to him,' said Dad ominously. Then he had one of his disastrous ideas. 'Hey! Why don't we invite him over this weekend, to help with the painting? I could make him an apple pie and he'll wonder what he ever saw in Miss Nose.' Touching though it was for Dad to volunteer to win back Fred's heart with pastry, Jess wished he'd back off and leave her personal life alone.

'Dad, stop!' yelled Jess. She had to stop him planning for tomorrow night right now. Letting things slide was a mistake – she was getting in deeper and deeper. She just had to summon all her courage and tell him it wasn't on, even if it broke his poor old arty-farty heart. 'I'm sorry, but tomorrow night's going to be a bit tricky for me,' she blundered recklessly, her mind racing.

'Tricky?' Dad looked troubled.

'I can't make it. I'm so sorry.' Dad looked disappointed, but Jess ploughed on. 'I can paint the bathroom with you tomorrow in the daytime, but in the evening I've got stuff to do.'

'What stuff?' asked Dad resentfully.

Jess had to think of some simply marvellous lies now. 'I've got a plan.' She lowered her voice, even though they were alone in the flat. 'It's to do with getting Fred back. You're right, of course. I – Flora and I – have a little scenario planned, and we think it's going to work.'

'What?' Dad sounded eager now, like a child wanting to be told a secret. 'Tell me all about it!'

'I can't!' Jess clenched her teeth with a massive lie-telling effort. Her chin must not wobble. She absolutely must not blush. 'The thing is, I feel if I tell you what the details are, I may jinx it.'

Dad nodded reluctantly. He was such a superstitious old hippy. 'Keep me posted, then,' he said. 'It doesn't involve throwing a wild party while Mum's away, I hope?'

'Oh no, no, of course not,' Jess reassured him hastily. She must not blush. She simply must not, *must not* blush. Oh no! She was blushing. Why was she blushing anyway? She wasn't holding a party. Having Flora and Jodie and Fred and maybe Mackenzie and Ben round for the evening – that wasn't a party. Jess encased both her cheeks in her hands, like somebody trying to hold their head together, which, in a way, was exactly what she was doing. Were her hands big enough to cover most of the blush? 'I'm going to be at Flora's. Don't breathe a word to Mum, though – she's got enough on her plate. If she asks, just pretend you and I are going to have a quiet weekend together, OK?'

Dad looked troubled and hesitant. He went over to the sink and started wiping down surfaces – a telltale sign that he was uneasy. 'I can't tell Mum an outright lie,' he said anxiously. 'I can't tell her you'll be here with me if you're not.'

'You won't have to!' Jess assured him. 'She'll be so busy ferrying Granny to the hospital and worrying about old Janie, she won't waste time thinking about me. And once the Fred business is all sorted I'll come over and see you on Sunday anyway.'

Dad looked doubtful, and Jess's heart sank. She was making a total mess of this.

'You must text me every hour with a progress report,' said Dad with a faint, encouraging smile. 'I'll be on tenterhooks.'

'Of course!' beamed Jess. 'And now, may I suggest the best cheesy omelette in history, followed by Scrabble?'

Chapter 9

Jess and Dad enjoyed a life-or-death Scrabble game, which he won at the very end, by putting down the word ZA. It was in *The Scrabble Dictionary*, but, in Jess's view, was not a proper word. Then Dad started to yawn and said he had to go to bed. Now he was working as a postman, he had to get up really early. He had a shift to do tomorrow morning, but he'd be back at two and then they could embark on the painting.

Jess could never, ever be a post-person. Staying up all night was far easier than getting up at dawn. She wondered for an instant whether if she'd been called Dawn, she'd have wanted to get up at dawn. Midnight was a better name for a girl, surely.

Settling down on Dad's sofa bed under the spare duvet was cosy and felt a bit like being on holiday. Jess switched on the TV and tried to focus on a romcom, but she couldn't really get into it. She had too much on her mind. If the gang were coming round for the evening, would she have to provide the entertainment? Fred could bring one of his blood-curdling DVDs. Should she text him to tell him? Or would it look as if it was just an excuse to contact him? But, then, when he'd come round to borrow the dictionary, was that just an excuse to see her? If so, giving him a black eye was hardly a tender and romantic form of hospitality. Jess cringed.

Suddenly, she was startled by a scratching at the window. Her blood froze. *Scrartle, scrartle, scrart!* What was this? The fingernails of a werewolf?

Jess shot from the sofa, tiptoed trembling to the window and bravely peeped through the curtains. Phew! It was only a tiresome tree tossing in the wind. The sky looked wild. It was going to be the kind of night when doors slam unexpectedly. Just as long as they didn't slam unexpectedly indoors. She was so tempted to run straight to Dad's room and seek shelter beneath his not-very-manly wing. But he had instructed her sternly not to interrupt him under any circumstances, as he was a very poor sleeper and was finding the early hours of a postman a strain after his cushy life as a kept man in St Ives.

Jess dived back under the covers and started planning her outfit for tomorrow night. For a quiet night in with her mates, she must be careful not to overdo it. Flora would be there, and Jodie and Fred. Mackenzie had more or less abandoned his idea of going to Devon, so he and Ben were bound to show up. Casual dress would be best, but what Jess needed was something casual and informal yet somehow so marvellous it would take Fred's breath away. The chance of finding something like that in her wardrobe was nil. Oh, for a fairy godmother who would wave her wand and transform Jess into a stunning beauty! Then she could wear any old thing and still look amazing.

Suddenly her phone pinged. Jess almost jumped out of her skin. It was a text from Fred!

WENT ROUND YOURS IN SECOND FUTILE ATTEMPT TO COLLECT DICTIONARY. HOUSE DESERTED. WHERE IS EVERYBODY?

Jess almost screamed aloud in frustration. Fred had gone round to see her again – and on a night when Mum and Granny had been out! The perfect opportunity for perhaps, who knows, a return bout of wrestling, which this time might have had a more delightful outcome. But instead of enjoying being home alone with Fred, Jess was trapped here in her dad's flat, condemned to a night of solitary *scrart*-ling.

And the wind was increasing. It was actually starting to moan in a *Wuthering Heights*-y sort of way. Outside, things were blowing about in the street. The window rattled as if a green-faced loon with long yellow teeth and empty eye sockets was trying to prise his way in.

What should she say in reply to Fred? *Hard cheese, old bean?* An impeccably vegetarian reply, though neither she nor Fred were vegetarians. *Sorry to miss the chance of inflicting a new injury?* In the end she settled for: AT DAD'S. SEE YOU TOMORROW. REMEMBER TO BRING GRUESOME DUDS. She was annoyed that she hadn't managed to think of a stylish joke, so for the time being she saved it as a draft. It wouldn't hurt to keep Fred waiting.

Suddenly there was the most terrific flash of lightning and a clap of thunder, and all the lights went out. The TV also popped into blackness. Jess's heart gave the kind of enormous leap that suggested it had once been the heart of a goalkeeper, then settled to a furious banging. It was at this moment, surely, that the green-faced loon would come sidling into the flat, possibly up through the loo.

Slowly, right on cue, the sitting-room door swung eerily open, with a stagy *creeeeak*! A tall, dark, shadowy figure glided in. Jess had grabbed a cushion when the wind had started moaning and now she sank her teeth into it.

'Are you all right, sweetheart?' It was Dad, of course. She'd known it was Dad. Sort of.

'Dad! Why did you have to come in so quietly and spookily? You should have come in doing a musical comedy routine, singing *Somewhere over the Rainbow*!'

'Sorry,' said Dad. 'I thought you might be asleep and I didn't want to wake you.'

'Dad, get a grip! I could never have slept through that thunder!'

'Of course, but are you OK?'

'OK? Sure! Why wouldn't I be?' Dad's concern was touching but somehow annoying, too.

'This storm is a bit melodramatic, isn't it?'

'Yeah. I'm not scared, though,' she lied. 'Don't worry.'

'I'm not, either,' said Dad, though he did sound a tad pale and shaky. 'Of course, on nights like this I really miss the crashing of the waves.'

'I know – wouldn't it be amazing if we were by the sea? Still, we'll have to make do with a boring town storm overlooking the dentist's car park. Any false teeth blowing about outside?'

'No. Anyway I just wondered if you were OK. Have

you been watching something scary on TV? I could bring my mattress in here and together we could fight off the Zombies of the Storm.'

Jess hesitated for a split second. She was so, so tempted to agree, though in any encounter between Tim Jordan and the Zombies of the Storm, the zombies would win hands down. 'I'm fine, Dad! Thanks, but I'm not frightened. And you're the one who's got to get up at five thirty or something.'

'Hmmm, OK. Maybe it's better to stay put. It's absolutely bucketing down now.'

'A positive hurricane, old bean.'

'OK, then. Well, goodnight. I'm so glad I tied the roof on with a bit of extra string last week.'

'Well done, Daddo – you think of everything.'

'Would you like a torch? There's one in the cupboard in the hall, I think.'

'No, Dad – it's fine. I'm cosied up on the sofa. I'll go straight off to sleep.'

'I'll just grope my way back to bed, then I expect the electricity will come on again any minute.'

'Course it will! Goodnight, Daddo!'

''Night, sweetheart!'

It seemed awfully lonely after Dad had gone back to bed. Jess lay on the sofa bed for a few minutes, trying to sleep, and then suddenly the electricity came back on with a big sigh as all the appliances started up again.

Jess looked around, staring at her discarded clothes strewn everywhere. On an odd impulse, she got up and started folding her stuff and making it tidy. Dad liked to have things just so, unlike Mum, who could get into a frenzy of clothes hurling, especially when packing. It wasn't so much that Jess wanted to earn brownie points; it was just that she wanted to be doing something while trying to work out how to rewrite the text to Fred. She felt restless.

Outdoors, the wind wailed, the rain lashed and the zombies encircled the building. Jess made sure all the windows and doors were locked, even though she knew perfectly well that zombies could probably sidle in through the keyhole or come swarming down the chimney.

Eventually she switched out the light, pulled the covers firmly over her head and stared at her mobile. What could she say to Fred? She had to send a message that was somehow, well, fabulous. But her mind was somehow, well, fabulously blank.

FRED, she wrote, THIS STUPID SITUATION IS DOING MY HEAD IN. HOW DO WE GET BACK TO THE WAY THINGS WERE? SUGGEST

WE CONSULT A WHITE WITCH FOR A SPELL TO TURN BACK TIME TO BEFORE THAT HORRIBLE VALENTINE'S DANCE. I HATE ST VALENTINE AND I HOPE HE WAS PAINFULLY MARTYRED. ALL MY LOVE FOR EVER, YOU COMPLETE SWINE. J XXX

Jess stared at this text for several minutes, her heart pounding, thinking how awful it would be if her finger slipped and she sent it. Carefully she deleted it and settled down to a night of wild wind and disturbing dreams.

Chapter 10

After waking up several times in the night, and having an exhausting nightmare about being chased by a small boy in school uniform who somehow had the teeth of a shark, Jess finally crawled out of bed at eleven thirty. Daylight is such a great invention; the storm was still blowing, but the zombies had fled. Dad had gone off for his Saturday morning shift sorting and delivering mail, leaving the kitchen spotless and a note confirming that he would be back at two, when they would go off and choose paint together. Jess could hardly wait.

She made herself some French toast, then had a long soaky bath and washed her hair. Dad's little flat had a cramped, poky bathroom with sickening orange walls, but the bath itself was five-star and there was loads of hot water – Jess was able to top up three times and read almost a hundred pages of *Gone with the Wind* (one of Dad's favourites).

Although quite wrinkly with watery soaking, as she dried herself she didn't entirely rule out having another bath when she got back home, because Fred would be coming this evening and it would be the first time they'd spent an evening in close proximity since the bust-up. She had to be massively fragrant even if she was going to be dressed, as usual, from head to toe in her charity-shop tat. Not that she was planning any significant moves. How could she? Fred and Jodie were an item, and Jess had to respect that. But if she was going to be marvellous, that had to include emitting a sublime fragrance.

She had finally thought of a text to send Fred. It was lame, certainly, but not half as lame as that needy blast of lurve she had come up with last night.

SORRY WAS OUT, she texted. ABDUCTED BY ALIENS. AM AT PRESENT ON PLANET THARG BUT THEY PROMISE TO GET ME HOME IN TIME FOR TONIGHT.

Satisfied, Jess had an hour to spend on her make-up before Dad came home.

'Wow! You're going to hit 'em for six in the paint shop!' he commented when he returned.

The paint shop was staffed by fat middle-aged men

in brown overalls. Jess had been hoping for something a little more glamorous, but it would have been hard to chat up a paint expert with Dad in the same room, so she abandoned her plans for a fragrant flirtation and instead found herself poring over the paint charts.

'Do you think white is a bit cold for a bathroom?' asked Dad, frowning at a chart which included some really nice soft pinky-whites.

'I'm torn between Piglet and Fresh Air,' pondered Jess. Paint colours have such weird names.

'I'm not sure, when I lie in the bath, if I want to be thinking about piglets or fresh air,' mused Dad. 'I fancy something a bit warmer, maybe on the gold side? Personally, I'm torn between Straw and Mittens.'

'Just think,' said Jess, smiling. 'Somebody's paid to think up these names. I fancy that job. The names are so random. Trilby! Why would a trilby be green?'

'Maybe if it was left out in the rain,' said Dad thoughtfully.

In the end they agreed on a pale blue, Dusk.

'Such a cliché to choose blue for a bathroom!' sighed Jess. 'If it was up to me I'd call this colour Flora's Eyes.'

'Sounds wonderfully romantic!' agreed Dad. 'The thing about blue, though, is that it doesn't have to be cold.'

Jess sensed a Tim Jordan Art Lecture looming. Sometimes her dad would go off on a flight of fancy when discussing colour – it had something to do with his being a painter, probably.

She felt her phone vibrate.

'Blue *can* be kind of warm,' Dad rambled on, still staring at various paint charts.

Jess whipped her phone out. The text was from Fred. Her heart lurched.

SORRY, WON'T BE ABLE TO MAKE IT TONIGHT. ALSO ABDUCTED BY ALIENS – THERE SEEM TO BE A LOT ABOUT THIS YEAR.

Jess's heart sank. Swiftly she pocketed the phone and stared blankly back at the paint charts.

'It all depends,' Dad continued, oblivious, 'on a lot of other things – whether there's a hint of something else in the mix and, above all, the kind of light in the room. I think this is a really nice blue, and the great thing is that the bathroom's south-facing.' He beamed at Jess, who nodded emptily.

OK, maybe it was a good thing in Parent-land that a bathroom faced south, but in the wreckage of her own private world, it hardly compensated for the sudden revelation that Jess's evening was going to be a Fred-free zone. It was mortifying to realise how much she'd been looking forward to Fred being there, and the way he'd ducked out of it – by using her own alien abduction idea against her – really hurt.

'So, Dusk it is, then?' asked Dad, looking down for her agreement. Poor Dad! In his book this was quality time with his darling daughter. It wasn't his fault her heart had turned to cardboard.

'Dusk – what could be more atmospheric? It's perfect, Daddo!' said Jess, managing a big smile.

Back at the flat, Jess hoped for an opportunity to slosh a lot of pale blue paint about, covering the previous tenant's Orange With A Hint of Sick. But Dad switched into Obsessive Painter Mode.

'Right,' he said sternly (by his standards), 'preparation is everything. First we have to wash the walls, then when they're dry we have to fill in all the cracks and then, when the filler's dry, we have to sandpaper it down so everything's nice and smooth.'

'But when are we going to get to the lovely painting?' wailed Jess.

'All in good time,' said Dad smugly and infuriatingly. 'Here's a sponge. You can wash the walls down. Make up a soapy solution in that bucket – washing-up liquid will do.'

'But, Dad, is this really necessary? I can't see any cracks in the walls and they look totally clean anyway.'

'You're so like your mum sometimes,' Dad reproached her with a satirical smile. 'Always in a rush. Never patient enough to do things properly.'

Reminded of Mum, Jess suddenly had a good idea: if she phoned Mum now and told her how she was helping Dad paint his bathroom, Mum would be less likely to phone tonight and disturb her evening with, well, with Flora probably, as Fred's absence no doubt meant that Jodie wouldn't be there, either. Mackenzie and Ben would probably show up if they hadn't got anything better to do, though. Mum had a knack for phoning right at the dramatic climax of films and asking Jess whether she was warm enough.

'Let's call Mum now!' she suggested, reaching for her phone.

'Call Mum when you've done the walls!' scolded Dad, pretending to be severe. 'And use the landline. You should save your mobile for emergencies only.'

Jess tried the landline, but Mum's phone went straight to voicemail.

'Hi, Mum!' Jess hesitated. 'Hope all's well. Hope Great-Aunt Jane is OK, and Granny. I'm at Dad's helping him paint his bathroom and tonight I'm, uh, going to Flora's, so see you tomorrow, I suppose . . . Lots of love!'

After washing the bathroom walls and watching Dad fill some cracks with white filler, Jess began to fidget.

'Dad, I have to go now. I need to go home and get ready for Flora's.'

'OK!' beamed Dad. 'Have a lovely time and make sure Fred comes to his senses.'

'Daddo!' Jess shook her head in amusement. 'Fred doesn't have any sense!'

And that was it – she escaped. But as she walked home, she didn't really feel liberated and excited. What was the point? An evening with Flora loomed, and that was fine, but when that evening had held the promise of Fred, the absence of Fred would sour everything. Even Fred with Jodie was better than no Fred at all.

Jess heaved a sigh. Oh, for the good old days when she and Fred had been inseparable! Now she had to pray for little glimpses of him across crowded rooms. And she was the one who'd dumped him. She felt really blue.

If she'd been naming blue paint for a living, she could have come up with a few beauties right now. Disappointment – a kind of pale, chilly blue with a hint of purple fingers, cold mornings and pointed silences. Desolation – a deep, tragic blue with a hint of divorce. Dejection – a midnight blue with a dash of cold, frosty, silvery, murderous steel and a hint of tooth-ache. She wasn't completely sure that she was suited to a career in advertising. That was more Jodie's style.

She was tempted to indulge in a Jodie diss-fest in the privacy of her own head, but she couldn't find the energy. Besides, she was supposed to be being marvel-lous all over the place and accepting how things were. It wasn't Jodie's fault she and Fred were an item. Fred could just have said no when Jodie rugby-tackled him to the ground and roared, 'Thou art mine!' He would never have been available for her if Jess hadn't decided to teach him a lesson. In reality, the person who'd been taught a lesson was herself.

Heaving a self-pitying mid-blue sigh with purple overtones, she fired off a text to Flora: LOOKS LIKE IT'S JUST YOU AND ME TONIGHT, SO SHALL WE JUST GET A PIZZA AND WATCH RANDOM TV?

Seconds later, just as she was walking up the front path and reaching for her key, a reply came back: JUST YOU AND ME? RU KIDDING? EVERYBODY'S COMING!

Chapter 11

Jess's heart missed a beat. Everybody? What did this mean? Did it include Fred? She raced indoors and dialled Flora's number.

'Flo! What do you mean? Who's everybody?'

'Oh, everybody! I mean, you know Mackenzie's not going to that thing down in Devon after all cos his parents totally freaked out about it, so he's coming to yours. Ben's coming, and I think Mackenzie's bringing a friend – Owen somebody.'

'What about . . . uh, Jodie and Fred?'

'Oh, they'll be there. Totally.'

'Fred sent me a text saying he wasn't coming because he'd been abducted by aliens.'

Flora laughed with a kind of mad delight. 'Oh, Fred's soooo funny!'

*That was **my** joke about the aliens*, thought Jess,

irritated – and irritated at herself for being irritated.

'Of *course* Fred's coming!' Flora went on. 'He was just kidding! You know Fred!'

But do I? Jess wondered. Although she and Fred had been inseparable for ages, right now she didn't have a clue what he was thinking. How happy was he with Jodie? Ecstatic or just so-so? Fred's world had become a mystery.

'Oh, right. Guess I'd better get a couple of pizzas out of the freezer, then.' Jess felt a lot more cheerful. She began to think about what to wear. 'Come early, Flo, OK? We can do our make-up together.'

'Right! I just have to finish my homework first.' At this remark of Flora's, Jess felt a guilty pang. She was nowhere near even starting her homework. 'So I'll be over around six thirty.'

'Sure! See ya then!'

Jess put down the phone. Could she transform herself into somebody traffic-stoppingly marvellous by tonight on a budget of precisely zero? Not exactly, but there might be something at the back of the wardrobe.

She raced up to her bedroom, ripped off her fleece and dived into a series of disastrous tops. The red flouncy number (too red), the leopard-print T-shirt (too tight), the rosebud smock (too ditzy and loose).

And then there was a lime-green plunging V-neck – no, it wasn't right. Her boobs Bonnie and Clyde were too, well, free range. Jess had had trouble with them once before, on the awful occasion when she'd made bra inserts out of plastic bags of minestrone soup for Tiffany's party. The memory of that horrendous evening still had the power to make her shudder. Staring at her reflection in the mirror now, she was glad she was a year older and wiser and wouldn't be wearing anything likely to cause a wardrobe malfunction.

This V-neck wasn't a suitable item of clothing for somebody marvellous – somebody with class and style – to wear. Jess took it off, hurled it to the floor and started to trawl through all her black clothing, of which there was enough to kit out a whole nation for a state funeral. Black was safe.

Eventually she settled on a black and white spotty top, hoping that if her clothing was tremendously spotty, her zits might seem more low-key. A plain black miniskirt, black tights and sparkly flats completed the ensemble. She looked, well . . . OK. If only she had a fashion-designer friend!

Eventually Flora arrived. Jess's jaw dropped. Flora had gone down the Hollywood route and was wearing a scarlet shift dress, bright red lipstick and killer heels.

'Flo, you look amazing!' gasped Jess. 'I look so lame next to you! I've got to change!'

'No, no!' insisted Flo. 'You look great!'

'No, I hate my look!' Jess argued. 'I'm a total frump! As usual, you're my role model! Come upstairs and help me transform myself!'

Jess raced upstairs to her bedroom and grabbed her only party number, the tiger-print dress with a metal studded collar. She kicked off her sensible flat shoes and wriggled into her patent killer heels. She had to wear heels, otherwise, standing next to Flora, Jess would look like a stunted, villainous hyena sizing up a glamorous giraffe.

'Come into the bathroom and help me with my make-up!' Jess was desperate for better lashes and more dramatic lippy. She hurtled along the landing, with Flora following a little more slowly, as she was consulting her phone.

'Mackenzie's bringing somebody called Morgan!' said Flora excitedly. 'He says she's awesome!'

Jess was half-delighted at the news and half-scared that Fred – if he did show up – might find Morgan a little too awesome. But she was too busy wiping off her previous make-up to spend much time fretting about a potential Morgan. She needed to vamp herself up, and fast.

'So, Flo . . .' she hesitated over her make-up box, '. . . which of these foundations, do you think?'

Just then the front doorbell rang.

'Go and let them in!' Jess was panicking now. 'I can't come down till my make-up's done! Go and hold the fort till I'm ready!'

Flora went down and Jess locked the bathroom door behind her. She didn't want anyone to barge in and catch her applying her seventh coat of lipgloss.

There was the sound of voices down in the hall; shrieks of laughter and some mad shouting. Jess didn't completely recognise the voices. One was obviously Mackenzie, but there seemed to be several people coming in. It was just like Mackenzie to bring a couple of friends. Bless him! He was such a party animal. Jess remembered that just a few hours ago she'd been feeling mid-blue and convinced her evening was going to be lonely and dull. Thank goodness for Mackenzie!

Hastily Jess slapped on her usual foundation. Normally she would have spent half an hour on her eyebrows, but that was clearly not going to be possible. The doorbell rang again. There was a buzz of conversation downstairs. Suddenly music blared out. It was so loud that the floor vibrated and the toothbrushes seemed to dance in their tumbler. Jess realised that she hadn't warned the people next door and, even worse, hadn't invited Luke. Not that she'd thought she was hosting anything worth inviting Luke to, but she appeared, unexpectedly, to be throwing a party.

The doorbell rang again. Jess grabbed her lipgloss. Her heart was pounding with excitement. She had to get downstairs and make a stylish appearance as the hostess with the mostest. One last tweak of the hair, one last slick of the lipgloss, and then Jess was ready to make her entrance. She opened the bathroom door and headed for the stairs.

Oh, horrors! The hall below was literally packed with bodies – living bodies, obviously – and though there were one or two people from their year group at school, Jess was basically looking down at a sea of strangers in her own home. She had a sudden urge to run. But how could she escape? Running off home wasn't an option. This *was* home. She had to stay and deal with it.

Chapter 12

Jess scanned the throng of strangers for a familiar face, but they were all strangers. There was a tall guy with ginger hair, a short fair guy with sticking-out ears, and a girl with shoulder-length hair and green glasses. Who on earth were all these people? A blonde girl with fluffy hair, wearing a satin miniskirt, was even now barging her way to the bottom of the stairs. Now she was coming up towards Jess, who was standing at the top of the stairs paralysed with uncertainty.

''Scuse me!' yelled the girl above the hubbub. 'Where's the loo?'

Speechlessly Jess pointed out the bathroom door, and the girl disappeared within, slamming it behind her. *Hey! Don't slam my bathroom door like that!* thought Jess. The girl hadn't even asked if she could use the bathroom. She hadn't even introduced herself. This was weird.

Jess plunged downstairs. She had to do *something*. She had to stop more people coming in. She had to find Mackenzie and ask him to sort this out. Oh no! There was the doorbell again, and now she was trapped in a heaving mass of bodies. Jess couldn't get to the front door to open it – or indeed lock it, which might have been the more sensible course of action. Somebody opened the door and three more complete strangers pushed their way in.

'Great party!' said somebody in her ear.

Jess turned and saw Tiffany, famous for her eyebrows as well as the party at which CCTV cameras had been concealed in the girls' loo. Tiffany lived in a palatial mansion flat, so they'd had separate 'Girlz' and 'Ladz' bathrooms. Jess's tiny house felt full to bursting already, and she had the awful feeling that more people could be arriving at any minute. Yes! There was the front doorbell again! Jess turned away from it in panic and decided to try and fight her way towards the kitchen.

Flora was there, talking to Mackenzie and Ben Jones. There was no sign of Fred or Jodie. There were about ten other people in the kitchen, only three of whom she had ever seen before. A tall plump boy with curly brown hair was pouring out drinks and handing them to people. It seemed as if the gate-crashers had brought enough food, drink and music for a party ten times as big as this tiny house would comfortably hold.

For a moment Jess was reminded of the time, quite recently, when she'd tried to squeeze herself into a pair of size-ten trousers. It just hadn't been possible. She had the same feeling now. The party was a size sixteen at least, while the house was a small size eight. Somebody opened the back door and a few people spilled out into the garden. This was good in a way because it created more space indoors, but it meant the noise of the party was spilling out, too – right under the windows of Luke's dad, who was Head of Sixth Form at St Benedict's!

Jess struggled across the kitchen to where her friends were pinned up against the dresser.

'Mackenzie!' shouted Jess. 'What *on earth* is going on? Are you responsible for this?'

'No, truthfully!' Mackenzie screamed in her ear. 'I only invited Peterson and Wood and Morris . . . and Owen Scott-Smythe and Morgan. Word must have got around. Still, it's a great party!'

'Who are these people?' yelled Jess. 'This is scary! It's out of control!'

'Relax!' shouted Mackenzie, with a not very convincing smile. 'Don't be such a control freak! OK, you don't know these people yet, but by the end of the evening you'll have a whole new bunch of friends!'

'By the end of the evening they could have totally trashed my house!' screamed Jess. The music was getting louder.

Flora laid a soothing hand on her arm. 'Don't worry, babe!' she said in Jess's ear. 'It'll be fine.'

Jess shook her head and glanced around in desperation. Complete strangers had taken over her house, and they didn't even seem to be aware it was hers. It was a horrible feeling. She pulled away from Flora and plunged back into the crowd. A girl with crooked teeth shrieked with laughter as she passed and spilled her drink on Jess's tiger-print dress.

'Oh, sorry!' the girl bawled. 'They probably have kitchen roll here, though!' It was weird and nightmarish to have her family referred to as 'they'.

Jess ignored the girl and pushed her way on through the hall. Somehow she needed to barricade Granny's room so nobody would go in there. It was sacred territory.

Too late. The door to Granny's room was open and – disaster! Four strangers were sitting in a line on

Granny's bed, taking photos of themselves on their mobiles and roaring with laughter. Jess was about to say something when three more people came in and greeted the others with wild delight and, in the process, Grandpa's framed photo got knocked off the bedside table. Luckily it didn't smash.

Jess dived and picked it up, then decided that upstairs was a safer option for this particular treasure. The hall was still packed with roaring and giggling strangers, the sitting room at the front was full of thudding noise, and several people had decided to sit on the stairs – a sign, thought Jess bitterly, of Very Low Intelligence and Extreme Bad Manners. She barged past them, ignoring their indignant remarks, and regained her precious first floor.

The first room was the tiny bedroom overlooking the garden where Mum slept. There was hilarious, out-of-control giggling and yelling coming from in there – the kind of sounds that you don't want to investigate. Then there was a queue for the bathroom, which included a girl she knew slightly called Jemma.

'Hey, great party, Jess!' she called, clutching gratefully at Jess's sleeve. 'Fabulous dress!'

Jess managed a feeble smile and pressed on. The next room was Mum's study, full of her books and papers. She opened the door and peeked in. A mock wrestling session was taking place on Mum's desk! Her papers were kind of scrunched-up underneath and would soon be ripped to shreds! But what could a hostess do? Shout, '*Stop that wrestling immediately and get off my mum's paperwork!*'? Hardly. If only she'd known she was going to be throwing a party, she could have put stuff away safely and locked a couple of doors – Granny and Mum's rooms, for a start.

On the verge of stressy tears, she barged into her own bedroom. There, sprawling on her bed, was her nemesis Whizzer – the boy who, at Tiffany's party, had squeezed her home-made bra inserts and caused a minestrone explosion. Two other boys and a girl were sitting on the floor, and the girl was cuddling Jess's teddy bear Rasputin, who stared at Jess with a look of total horror and outrage on his dear old face.

'Excuse me!' said Jess – a little stroppily (though nobody noticed). 'I want to put this in a safe place.'

She went across to her bedside table and pulled the drawer open. Annoyingly, a bra popped out.

Whizzer made a stupid whooping noise. 'So, lovely Jordan, this is your hideaway, is it?' He grinned, grabbing her wrist.

'Let go!' yelled Jess, wrenching herself free with

such panache that the photo of Grandpa went flying out of her hand and crashed violently into her mirror. There was a splintering sound as the glass of the photo frame smashed and the mirror also cracked. Jess screamed.

'Oh no!' yelled the girl. 'Seven years' bad luck!'

Seven years! The awful repercussions of this party were surely going to last a lot longer than that, and Jess felt that the bad luck had already started – in spectacular fashion.

Chapter 13

'I'll go and get a dustpan and brush,' said Jess through clenched teeth. She placed the splintered photo frame carefully on her desk. 'Don't touch anything!' she warned, giving Whizzer a stern look.

'Don't worry, we won't nick anything!' Whizzer grinned. 'But where d'you keep your love letters?'

'Shut up, you idiot!' Jess snapped and headed for the door.

'Ooooooh!' cried Whizzer in a high, girly scream. 'Temper, temper!'

'Shut up, Whizzer!' said the girl. She seemed to be a decent person, though for her to cuddle Rasputin without being introduced was a bit of a cheek.

Jess needed a padded envelope. That was the way her mum always dealt with broken glass: she'd wrap it in newspaper, then seal it up with tape 'so it doesn't cut the bin men'. Out in the garden shed was a box of old newspapers waiting to be recycled and a collection of plastic carrier bags – everything she needed!

She struggled downstairs, past about five more intruders, then barged through the crowds in the hall and kitchen, and burst out of the back door into the night. Even her garden was full of strangers, and the noise was embarrassingly loud. She looked at Luke's house – the downstairs lights were on. She knew it would only be a matter of time before his dad came round to complain.

A couple of guys out in the garden were pretending to dance the tango. They tripped and fell, landing heavily right on Mum's beloved daffodils.

'Hey, you!' yelled Jess. 'Get off those flowers! Show some respect!'

There were some sniggers and a half-hearted 'apology' (you could almost hear the inverted quotes in their tone) and the group went back indoors. Jess approached the garden shed. *Please, God*, she prayed, *let there be nobody in here*.

Bliss! It was empty. Jess collected a handful of newspapers and three carrier bags and began the arduous journey back up to her room. One or two people greeted her or said things like 'Amazing party!', but she ignored them. This wasn't a party. This was an invasion.

Back up in her room, she found Whizzer and co cracking up about something – Jess didn't know what exactly but she felt somehow that they were laughing at her. As Whizzer imitated her strict headteacher-ish voice, Jess could easily imagine that he'd made fun of her, too, the moment she'd left the room.

She laid the newspaper down on her desk and picked up the shattered photo frame.

'Can I help?' asked the girl, getting up and throwing Rasputin down on the bed. *Throwing* Rasputin! Jess almost screamed aloud at this insult to her bear, but she obviously couldn't say anything – not unless she wanted to sound like a five-year-old.

'It's all right, thanks,' she replied with chilly haughti-ness. 'It's just my granny's photo of Grandpa which some clumsy idiot smashed.'

'Hey!' cried Whizzer. 'You were the clumsy idiot who smashed it, remember?'

'I wouldn't have smashed it if you hadn't grabbed me in your usual charming way,' snarled Jess.

'Just trying to be friendly,' sniggered Whizzer. 'What's up with you?'

Jess ignored this remark. Examining the photo sadly, she could see that she would probably have to buy a whole new frame. How easy was it to buy replacement glass? Tomorrow was a Sunday, so it would be virtually impossible. Granny was sure to notice, but then the whole house was going to be a wreck.

Carefully she disposed of the glass, removed Grandpa's photo from the frame and put it in her wardrobe. As she opened the wardrobe, Fred's face looked up at her. All her photos of Fred were stashed away out of sight. She'd found it too upsetting to be reminded of happier times and his range of diabolical and silly expressions. Hastily she closed the wardrobe door and locked it.

Where was Fred? Maybe he wasn't coming after all. Maybe he'd heard that it was going to be a massive party and had just quietly stayed at home. That would be so like Fred. He hated parties – allegedly. Lying on the sofa watching horror films was his idea of a fun evening. Loud music wasn't his sort of thing, either. Fred's way of interacting with people was via jokes, and in this racket you could hardly make yourself heard by shrieking in somebody's ear. It was a bit quieter up here in her bedroom, but the presence of the vile Whizzer cancelled out any benefit. If he hadn't been around, Jess might just have locked herself in her bedroom and stuck her head under the pillow until the nightmare was over.

But it really was her responsibility to deal with this, even though she hadn't invited these people. She had to get rid of them, so she began a fruitless search for somebody she could ask to help her.

Once again she moved through every room in the house. Her mum's study had been vacated by the wrestlers and now there were four people in there, sitting on the floor playing cards.

Eventually Jess reached the kitchen and, in the far corner, she saw, with a leap of her heart, that Fred had arrived. He and Ben Jones had joined Flora, who was chatting to a tall good-looking guy. Only the best for Flora! There was no sign of Jodie. Fred was in the middle of some entertaining monologue and didn't notice her, but Ben Jones caught Jess's eye across the room. He looked concerned.

Jess headed for them like somebody floundering through quicksand. At last she reached the little group. It had never taken so long just to walk across her kitchen.

'Ben! Fred!' she yelled across the din. 'Can I have a word – outside – please?'

They escaped to the garden, which, miraculously, was having an empty moment.

'This is terrible!' Jess felt her voice wobble and her legs start to shake. 'Who are these people? They're trashing my house! The neighbours will be round in a minute! Where's Mackenzie? I'm going to kill him! We've got to get rid of everyone!'

'I could ask them politely to leave,' said Fred in a droll voice which totally disregarded her real pain, 'but I'm not sure they'd hear me.'

'Call the police?' ventured Ben.

'Don't!' screamed Jess. 'That would make it worse! And anyway, I expect somebody's called the police already! This is a nightmare! Do something!'

'What would make them go?' pondered Fred, looking at Ben. 'What do they need . . . really need?' He cudgelled his brains, trying at last to focus on the problem. 'Hey!' He clapped his hands in a moment of sudden divine revelation. 'Got it! Electricity! Like the power cut last night! Where's your electricity meter?'

'Under the stairs,' said Jess. 'In that dark little cupboard.'

'I could crawl under there and switch it off!' said Fred. 'That would stop the music and everything.'

'But would they leave?' wailed Jess. 'There are

people all over the house. They might just carry on. In fact, they might prefer it dark.'

'We could, uh, tell them the police are coming!' said Ben suddenly.

'Brilliant! Brilliant!' Fred beamed. 'But also, if we tell them there's another party somewhere, they'll go off there.'

'Where?' asked Jess. 'I want them well away from here.'

'In the town centre,' suggested Fred. 'At the corn exchange or the leisure centre!'

'No . . .' Ben hesitated. 'Somebody here's bound to know what's really happening in town tonight. It's got to be a, like, private party.'

'At a false address!' added Fred excitedly. '26 Park Avenue! Sounds chic!'

'It can't be completely false,' warned Jess. 'They've got to know where they're going or they'll just hang around here.'

'How about one of those posh streets with big houses?' said Fred. 'Like, you know, Tiffany's place. What's it called? Bedtime Circus or something?'

'Bedford Crescent,' said Ben.

'Right,' said Fred. 'I'll turn the electricity off . . . How do you do that, by the way? Preferably without killing yourself?'

'I'll turn the electricity off,' said Ben, confident for once. 'I've done it loads of times. You'd better shut me in that cupboard so nobody comes poking their nose in trying to fix it. The minute the lights go off, you start shouting about the police coming and the alternative party in Bedford Crescent. OK?'

'OK,' agreed Fred. 'And let's try and get Mackenzie to do the shouting, too. Where is he?'

'Don't waste time looking for Mackenzie,' said Jess. 'I have plans for him. He's going to spend the rest of his life cleaning the floors of my house with his tongue.'

Chapter 14

Ben Jones was taking control of the situation and, mysteriously, he seemed to have been transformed from a hesitant, if glamorous, bystander into a go-getting superhero. Well, the nearest thing available locally.

They disappeared into the house and moments later it was plunged into darkness. The music stopped abruptly, but the shocked silence didn't last long; it was replaced by screams and giggles and wisecracks. Above it all Jess could hear Fred yelling, 'Party at Bedford Crescent! Everyone invited! Disco! Bedford Crescent, everyone! Let's go!'

Jess had been lingering in the garden, the only part of her home which still seemed to belong mostly to her, but now she felt she should join the effort to evict her unwelcome guests.

'Jess?' said a man's voice, close by in the dark.

Jess almost jumped out of her skin. A pale face was looking at her across the fence.

It was only Luke's dad, Mr Appleton. He looked ever so slightly annoyed. 'What's going on, Jess? If I'd known you were going to have a party I'd have gone out for the evening.'

'Oh, Mr Appleton, I'm so, so sorry!' gushed Jess, uneasily aware that her plan to keep this event a deep dark secret from Mum was going to be virtually impossible if Mr Appleton knew all about it, as he often dropped in for a coffee and they indulged a mutual love of gossip, going at it hammer and tongs for hours. 'Everybody's leaving now – we're getting rid of them. We've turned the power off, you see.'

'Did your party get a bit out of hand, then?' asked Mr Appleton, not completely without sympathy.

'It wasn't my party!' insisted Jess. 'I never intended to have a party! It was originally going to be just Fred and Jodie and Flora and me watching a DVD and having a pizza. Only four of us! These people just gatecrashed. I don't even know who they are.' Jess wished she wasn't wearing her tiger-print dress and killer heels, as they did sort of suggest that she was intending to have a party.

'I've heard about this sort of thing,' said Mr Appleton anxiously. 'I think word gets around on Facebook or something. Once it starts it's hard to stop. It builds up a kind of momentum. Can I help you get these people out? Shall we ring the police?'

At this crucial moment in neighbourly relations, Jess's mobile rang.

'Oh, excuse me . . .' she faltered.

It was Dad! What a time to ring! He thought she was at Flora's!

If only Mr Appleton would go back indoors, but instead he loitered by the fence in an eavesdropping kind of way. He probably thought he was being supportive. In fact, he was being about as supportive as a carrier bag full of cow dung hurtling towards your head.

'Hi, Jess!' said Dad cheerfully. 'How's it going? Has Fred done the decent thing and dumped that girl with the nose?'

'Dad, relax! These things take time!' said Jess, instantly cursing herself for calling him Dad and therefore revealing to Mr Appleton that her father was on the phone.

She tried to stroll semi-casually towards the garden shed and away from Mr Appleton a little, in case he vaulted lightly over the fence and cried, *'Is that your father? Let me speak to him! This calls for a Dads United Show Of Strength! We'll drive these interlopers from your house with our golf clubs, and afterwards we'll give you a stern talking-to for being so useless as to let them in in the first place!'*

Unfortunately, at this moment, a small group of people who thought they were being hilarious came tumbling out of the dark kitchen and fell in a heap at Jess's feet, howling.

'What on earth is that noise?' asked Dad.

'Oh, it's just a movie,' said Jess, moving hastily down the garden away from the hilarious gatecrashers. 'Flora's got a great collection. I must go actually, Dad. There's a pizza in the oven and I can smell it starting to burn.' She muttered this last lie into the phone as privately as possible so Mr Appleton wouldn't hear, and Jess felt briefly, unexpectedly grateful to the guys who were still howling in a heap.

'OK, well, enjoy your evening,' said Dad.

'And enjoy yours, Daddo. What are your plans?'

'I thought I'd just pop over to Mum's to use her internet so I can check my emails,' said Dad. 'Mine's stopped working since that power cut last night.'

Nightmare! In a minute Dad was going to turn up

right here and the house was comprehensively trashed and still half-full of strangers! Jess's heart lurched into a series of giddy somersaults.

'No! Wait!' she cried. 'I can come over to yours and fix it! I know what to do – you just have to enter a few codes!'

'Thanks, love, but I wouldn't want to ruin your evening,' said Dad tenderly – ruining it comprehensively anyway, the idiot. 'I might as well go over to Mum's because I'm going to bake some muffins and I think she's got buttermilk.'

Oh, why, why, why had fate given her a dad who was gay? Up until now Jess had been proud and pleased to have such a stylish parent, but now she realised there were disastrous side effects. Muffins, indeed! Why couldn't he watch football on TV on a Saturday night, like most people's dads? His flat was only a ten-minute stroll away. How could she possibly detain him?

Fred burst out of the back door. 'Party at Bedford Crescent!' he yelled. 'Disco! Barbecue! Karaoke! Oh, hello, Mr Appleton.'

'Who are you?' asked Mr Appleton, peering through the dark.

'Forget Bedford Crescent!' roared a partygoer. 'I like it here!'

'Jess!' said Dad in her ear. 'What's going on?'

'Just – nothing!' said Jess hastily. 'Don't bother to go to Mum's. I'll be leaving Flora's in a minute and I can bring the buttermilk over and sort your internet out.'

'But you said you were just about to have a pizza,' said Dad. He was beginning to sound suspicious and a little cross. Even landscape painters have their limits. Dad did occasionally lose his temper, about once every three years. The red mist would descend and, because he was a painter, it could be anything from Scarlet Lake to Rose Madder (when he was really furious it was Rose Madder, naturally).

'But, Dad, this evening's not going very well. I feel like coming round to yours anyway. I'll explain when I get there.'

'Let's meet at Mum's instead,' said Dad firmly. 'I promised her I'd look in on the house to make sure everything's OK. See you there.' And he rang off, without even saying 'love you' or any of his usual jokey endearments. Jess's blood ran cold. Dad was on his way and was already suspicious and grouchy!

'My dad's coming!' shouted Jess to the people trampling on Mum's daffodil patch. There was no need to tell them he was a landscape painter who was afraid of the dark. At the thought of a dad coming, they began to look as though they were going to make a move.

Fred, meanwhile, had gone over to the fence and was chatting to Mr Appleton.

'Did I hear you say your father's coming, Jess?' called Mr A.

You heard the whole freaking lot, Big Ears, thought Jess, perhaps a tad ungratefully.

'Yes, he's coming,' said Jess. 'So he can lay down the law if necessary.'

'Oh, good,' said Mr Appleton. 'Well, if he needs reinforcements, don't hesitate to come and get me.'

'Thanks so much! And I'm so sorry about the noise!' Jess wrung her hands apologetically and put on a sickeningly ingratiating smile. Anything to get Mr Appleton back inside his house.

'Right,' said Fred. 'Guys, there's an emergency exit down here! You don't want to meet Jess's dad when he's in a temper – he punched a hole in the kitchen wall last time he got angry!'

Fred led them down the garden to an overgrown old door in the back wall and, heaving it open with a huge effort, he shooed them out into the lane. Dear Fred! He was doing his best to help. But Jess hadn't got time to thank him right now. She had to empty the house before Dad arrived.

The noise from the house was dwindling and suddenly the lights came on again. Had Ben switched them back on too soon? Would the restoration of electricity make people want to stay? Jess rushed indoors.

'My father's coming!' she shouted. 'Quick! Quick! He's in a rage! You've got to leave!'

A few people who had been standing around in the kitchen looked quite alarmed and headed for the front door. The hall was almost clear. Jess glanced swiftly into Granny's room. It was empty, though the window was open and the carpet was covered with half-eaten food. A huge bottle of Coke had toppled over and leaked a dark pool of drink all over Granny's precious rug. Jess's heart sank. It would take hours to get Granny's room looking respectable again, and the kitchen was a sea of trash.

She ran back into the kitchen, where Flora was still chatting to her tall and handsome friend.

'Quick, Flo!' shouted Jess irritably. 'My Dad's coming! Clear this kitchen! Quick!'

Flora looked startled but put down her glass. The guy she was talking to reached for his coat.

Jess ran off to the sitting room. Three people were in there.

'Sorry, but you have to go!' shouted Jess. 'My dad's coming and he'll go ballistic! He's called the police already!'

'Chill!' said one guy. 'We're not criminals, OK?'

Jess didn't stay to argue the case. She raced upstairs to check the other rooms. There were just a few last stragglers, and at the fearful news that a timid gay landscape artist called Tim was on his way to wreak terrible vengeance on the gang who had trashed his librarian ex-wife's home, they fled.

Jess ended up in her own bedroom. It didn't look quite as bad as the other rooms, but that was only because she kept it in a semi-trashed state all the time. Where was Rasputin? Oh no! He was definitely missing! That wretched girl must have nicked him! At the thought that her beloved bear had been kidnapped, Jess burst into tears – tears which had been waiting for their chance all evening. She was halfway through her first salvo of sobbing when she heard her dad's voice down in the hall.

'What in the name of Sacred Nora has been going on here? Jess? Where are you? JESS!'

Chapter 15

Jess hastily kicked off her high heels and wriggled back into her flats, then she went downstairs, dabbing at her eyes with a tissue.

Dad was standing in the hall, staring up at her. He looked pale and shocked. Jess turned up the volume of her sobbing ever so slightly and, reaching the bottom of the stairs, launched herself determinedly into Dad's arms. This instantly put him at a disadvantage, as he was such an awkward amateur when it came to hugging, but he cooperated to a certain degree, not actually hurling her off or shouting, '*Let me go, you treacherous child! You promised me you weren't going to have a party while Mum was away and look at this mess!*' This was the very least that Flora's dad would have done.

'Dad! Dad! It was awful!' she sobbed, overtaken by genuine feelings of shock and horror. This had been a real nightmare – for several hours she had been over-whelmed with a horrendous sense that she had completely lost control of her life. 'This gang of people just turned up and took over the house! They were total strangers!'

'Somebody must have started it,' said Dad. 'The word must have got around somehow that you were giving a party. And you promised me yesterday that you weren't!' Dad wriggled out of the hug and held her at arm's length, staring solemnly into her face.

Jess cringed. 'I really wasn't giving this party! I wasn't, honestly, Dad! It was forced on me! The only thing I'd planned was a quiet evening in with Flora and maybe Fred and Jodie, watching DVDs and having pizzas.'

'But you told me you were going to Flora's! I was on the phone ten minutes ago and you told me then you were at Flora's.'

'I'm sorry, but by then I was panicking! And anyway, yesterday I did think I was going to Flora's!' This was hardly five-star lying or apologising, but it was the best Jess could manage in her present frazzled state.

At this opportune moment Flora drifted into the hall, carrying a black bin bag half-full of debris.

'We were originally planning to get together at your house, weren't we, Flo?'

Flora hesitated, probably because she couldn't remember which pack of lies they had been telling yesterday. 'That's right,' she said. 'We were.'

'So why did you change your plans?' demanded Dad, unusually forcefully. Jess wondered for a split second if he'd just been on an Assertiveness Training Course.

'Because my dad said he didn't want people round,' said Flora, lightly leaping into her lying mode.

Jess had noticed that, ironically, when Flora was lying, her left eyebrow tilted slightly towards heaven. It was tilting now, big time. Luckily Dad hadn't spent any time studying Flora's lying habits and, in any case, was bound to accept her version of events more readily than Jess's just because she wasn't his daughter.

'He's a bit grumpy at the moment and he said he didn't want his house full of kids,' Flora went on, gaining confidence from the fact that this was, by and large, a perfectly honest version of what her dad said at least three times a week. 'And my mum wasn't feeling very well, either,' Flora added. 'She had a sore throat so she wanted an early night. We decided it would be best to come to Jess's because her mum and granny were away, so they wouldn't be disturbed.'

'Not that we were planning to do anything loud,' Jess agreed vehemently.

'So how come these people – these gatecrashers – thought you were giving a party?'

There was an awkward pause, during which Jess could hear Fred and Ben's voices as they moved furniture about upstairs – presumably clearing up, bless them!

'I think it was Mackenzie,' said Flora, blushing guiltily as she dumped her former heart-throb in it. 'He invited three friends, I think. Owen Scott-Smythe – that guy I was talking to in the kitchen. And Jamie Peterson and Harry Wood. And maybe one more person. Maybe they put the word about that there was going to be a party.'

'And where is this Mackenzie character?' asked Dad, looking grim.

Jess shrugged. 'I haven't seen him recently,' she said. 'Have you?' She turned to Flora, who shook her head.

'Ben said he began to freak out when more and more people came,' said Flora, 'so he made some lame excuse about not feeling well and headed home.'

Fred and Ben Jones came downstairs at this point, carrying bin bags and a bucket and mop.

'We need a vacuum cleaner,' said Ben.

'Oh, hi, Mr Jordan,' said Fred. 'I'm really sorry you have to see the house like this. Don't worry, we'll work all night if necessary to clean it up before Jess's mum comes back.' Fred looked really serious. It was odd to see him not being funny.

'What a mess,' Dad sighed and made a move towards the kitchen.

Jess sensed that her confrontation with him was over and that now he wanted to take the tour. While Fred, Ben and Flora attacked the kitchen, Jess and her dad trudged miserably from room to room, inspecting the whole house. Despite the early efforts of the home team, the place still looked terrible, and smelt worse.

Dad was a tidy man. In his own immaculate home, just seeing the waste-paper basket placed a fraction too near the TV could send him spiralling into depression.

Mum's study was a priority because her paperwork had been wrestled on.

'Don't get rid of any of that paperwork. It could be important,' warned Dad. 'We can probably salvage it.'

'How?' asked Jess hopelessly, staring at the chaos.

'We can wash it, dry it and iron it,' said Dad. 'Some

of these papers won't need such drastic treatment, though. Just ironing them will be enough.'

'But will they look as good as new?' asked Jess fretfully. 'Will Mum realise that something's happened? I really, really don't want to tell her what happened here tonight, if at all possible.'

Dad turned to Jess and gave her a very dry, sceptical look. 'Oh, you can't hope to hide this from Mum,' he said, with a nasty bitter little laugh that had absolutely no humour in it. 'Believe me, Jess, she has to know about this.'

Jess's heart sank with furious speed, like an anchor plummeting through fathoms of icy water to a dark and cheerless seabed, where things with monstrous green eyes crawled among slimy weeds and rocks. She was in the biggest trouble ever, and she couldn't even work out whether it was her fault or not.

At this point, curiously, her mobile rang.

Chapter 16

It was Jodie. 'Hey, Jess! I just rang Fred to ask how the evening was going and he told me about the invasion! I'm so, so sorry I can't be there to help you clean up!'

'Oh, that's OK,' replied Jess, slightly puzzled. Why wasn't Jodie over here anyway? Why hadn't she come with Fred?

'I'm stuck on the sofa for the next few days,' said Jodie. 'I wish I could have been there! I'd have chased those gatecrashers away! You could have released me like a Staffordshire bull terrier! Fred often says I can snap and growl for England!'

Ignoring for a moment this interesting quotation from Fred, Jess went back to the mysterious reference to the sofa. 'Why are you stuck on the sofa for the next few days?' she asked.

'Didn't Fred tell you? I pulled a hamstring when we were out running this afternoon. What a nightmare! I can't even walk now, let alone run. I'll never make the half-marathon. I'll have to ask all my sponsors if they'll sponsor Fred instead. I'm absolutely gutted.'

'Oh, Jodie, I'm so sorry! I didn't know.'

'Fred didn't mention it, then?' Jodie sounded slightly edgy at this point.

'No, but, then, I've hardly seen him all evening. All these people arrived, and I was just kind of blown away by it, you know. I was totally unprepared. But I'm really, really sorry to hear about your hamstring. How long will it take to get better?'

'It's gonna be weeks,' moaned Jodie. 'Three days' total rest first, plus my mum is taking me to the physio on Monday. Then in the second week I'll be able to come back to school – maybe earlier, but it could be a month before I'm fit to trot again.'

Jess felt really sorry for Jodie. 'You poor thing!' she said. 'I'll come round and see you tomorrow.'

'Would you, Jess?' asked Jodie eagerly. 'Oh, that would be ace! I'm so bored lying here with my leg up.'

'Sure!' Jess promised. 'I just have to clear up the mess here, which should only take, uhhh, a hundred years.'

'Oh, Jess, that's awful!' cried Jodie. 'You poor thing.'

'It's OK,' Jess told her. 'Ben is here and Flora and Fred and my dad. But Mackenzie's scarpered.'

'Hah!' snorted Jodie in a jokey way. 'Fred! He'll be *loads* of help, I'm sure.'

She was wrong, though. Fred found some carpet shampoo and set to work on Granny's sacred rug. Dad worked on restoring Mum's study to some kind of order. He took the ironing board up there and for the next hour or two he could be seen rinsing papers, hanging them up to dry and then pressing them. Flora and Ben concentrated on the kitchen and sitting room, collecting rubbish, rinsing cans for recycling, washing glasses and generally scrubbing and polishing.

'How's the rug coming along?' said Jess, dropping in on Fred in Granny's room.

'It's fine,' said Fred. 'I've always wanted to shampoo a carpet, but my mum always said I'd have to wait till I was eighteen. Weird word, isn't it? Sham-poo. Sounds, well, sounds like something else. You know the plastic dog poos in joke shops? When I was at primary school, we put one under Mrs Porter's desk. When she saw it she just picked it up and put it in her pocket. Some of the girls screamed, but she ignored them. She was as cool as anything. She didn't even try to find out who had put it there. We had to wait till break to laugh about it and then we all wet ourselves.'

Fred seemed to be talking too much, jabbering nervously rather than just occasionally serving up witty asides in his usual cool style.

'Delightful memories,' quipped Jess. 'Remind me never to be a primary school teacher.'

'So what are your current career plans, Jordan?' asked Fred, putting on a posh headmaster's voice.

'Well, after tonight's big success I'm thinking of becoming an events organiser,' said Jess. 'In my experience, you just have to sit back and do nothing and things will happen by themselves. What are your plans?'

'I'm going to be a carpet shampooer,' said Fred, squeezing foam off his sponge and scattering it lightly in all directions. 'I like a job where you can kneel down. I was planning to take holy orders but I don't want to be called Father. Even if I have children, I want them to call me Dave.'

'Why didn't you tell me Jodie had injured her leg?' asked Jess suddenly. The question had been hiding behind her face for several minutes and now it had sort of taken its chance and burst out.

Fred seemed to freeze for a second mid-shampoo

and looked at the wall. 'Oh, yes,' he said absent-mindedly. 'I forgot about that. Well, there was so much going on here.'

Several contrasting feelings flooded through Jess's heart. It was kind of bad of Fred to have forgotten about poor Jodie's injury, but in a way Jess was secretly pleased about it. She didn't like the fact that she felt slightly pleased, though. She was ashamed of that feeling. What if she was the one who'd injured her leg and Fred had forgotten about her? Back in the days when they'd been an item, obviously.

'How did it happen?' she asked. 'Did she fall down or something?'

'No, she was just, well, running along as usual – way up ahead of me, of course – and I saw her pull up and feel the back of her thigh. She's out for three or four weeks.'

'Did she manage to walk home?' persisted Jess. For some reason she wanted to know every detail . . . Had Fred helped her home? Had he carried her? Had he gone with her to Casualty? Had he held her hand?

'She rang her dad, and he came to collect her.' Fred shrugged. 'He took her off to a clinic or something. She sent me a text saying it's a grade two pull, whatever that means. If it's a grade three apparently you need surgery. I told her to try harder next time.'

'I'll go and see her tomorrow,' said Jess. 'I'll take her some DVDs.'

She hesitated. She was tempted to ask Fred to go with her, but that might be a bit weird. Fred and Jess turning up together as if . . . He might be there at Jodie's anyway. After all, he was supposed to be Jodie's boyfriend, even if he'd forgotten all about her injury – or pretended to forget about it. Everything was so complicated. If only she knew what he was thinking.

'She won't be able to do the half-marathon, then,' Jess went on. 'She sounded gutted when I spoke to her.' She watched Fred dabbing away at the rug with his sponge. 'She said she's going to have to ask all her sponsors to sponsor you instead – is that right?'

Fred sat back on his heels and sighed. He rinsed his sponge in the bucket and squeezed it. 'I was hoping we could cancel the whole thing now,' he said. 'It was madness right from the start.'

'It wasn't madness!' cried Jess. 'It was a really, really good thing to do! You've got to stick with it!'

Fred shrugged and looked uncooperative. 'I suppose I have to,' he agreed. 'Unless I can somehow manage to pull my own hamstring. Or maybe you could pull it for me?'

Jess felt they were treading very carefully around some really dodgy subjects now.

'That would be chic,' she observed drily. 'Matching hamstring injuries – for the couple who have everything.'

Fred locked eyes with her for a moment, and his expression was tormented. For once, Jess was glad that he hadn't laughed at one of her jokes.

Chapter 17

This was bizarre! Jess felt her heart lurch and she longed to reach out to Fred. But that would be wrong, so very wrong. It was bad enough that poor Jodie was stuck on her sofa, in awful pain. The last thing she needed now was any trouble on the relationship front. After all, Jess had dumped Fred, and for a good reason . . . though as time passed she was beginning to think she might have overreacted.

Still, she couldn't think about that now. She needed to move the conversation away from any dodgy areas. She turned to Granny's crumpled bed. Jess began to remake the bed, then discovered that somebody had spilled a can of Coke all over the sheets.

'Oh no, look at this!' she sighed. 'Mackenzie's friends really gross me out.'

'I'm not sure Mackenzie should take the blame,'

said Fred, getting up. 'Although, obviously, he's much more to blame than, say, me. As you know, I hate parties.'

'Why did you come, then?' asked Jess, pulling the stained sheets off the bed. Fred helped her in an awkward fumbling way.

'I didn't know it was going to be a party,' said Fred. 'I thought it was just going to be DVDs and stuff. Just you and Flora and whoever. I wasn't even in the mood to talk. As you know, I hate talking. I hate talking and I hate people. I'm going to be a paving stone in my next life.'

'Shut up and pass me that pillowcase,' demanded Jess. Fred struggled to get the case off the pillow.

'In fact,' he went on, 'I feel that talking was always going to be a mistake. I think Homo sapiens took a wrong turn when we were evolving.'

'What should we have done, then?' asked Jess. 'Singing? That would have been great. Imagine a newsreader singing the news.'

'Yeah. Or you go to the doctor – "*What seems to be the troooouuuble?*"' Fred warbled the line, operatic style.

'Football commentary would be better sung,' observed Jess. 'I suppose it already is, sometimes:

Gooooooooooooal! So, how do you think we should have evolved instead?'

'Flying,' said Fred firmly. 'It's the only way to travel! Wings instead of arms.' He flapped his about. 'I'd like to be an albatross.'

'Why don't you plan to be one in your next reincarnation, then?' suggested Jess. 'It sounds like a lot more fun than being a paving stone.'

'Yeah, and the way albatrosses fly is cool, too,' said Fred. 'They just glide about for hours and hours without any effort.'

'Ah, your perfect lifestyle!' commented Jess ironically. 'Now I'm going to put Granny's sheets in the washing machine and get some clean ones. You can help me remake the bed.'

'Wow, what a treat!' commented Fred, picking up the carpet shampoo bucket. 'I bet albatrosses never have to make a bed.'

They went into the kitchen, where Flora was mopping the floor and Ben Jones was drying some glasses.

'Thanks so much, guys!' said Jess, feeling a rush of gratitude. 'At times like this you certainly find out who your friends are.'

'We're nearly done here,' said Flora. 'Then Ben's

going to vacuum upstairs and I'm going to clean the bathroom.'

'How can I ever repay you?' asked Jess, tipping the sheets into the washing machine.

'Cash is fine,' said Fred. 'Or a couple of gold bars would be ideal.'

'This is nothing,' said Flora, wringing the mop out into the sink. 'I quite like cleaning, actually. I think I might be a cleaner when I leave school.'

'After your brilliant career at Oxford and your first-class degree in maths, I presume?' Jess smiled.

'But cleaning is so satisfying,' sighed Flora, putting the mop away in the cupboard. 'Look at that floor! Nobody must step on it, though, or I'll have a nervous breakdown.'

'So we'll have to stay in our present positions for all eternity.' Jess grinned.

'Suits me fine.' Fred jumped up and sat on one of the kitchen units, his long legs swinging to and fro.

Ben Jones, leaning against the cooker, said nothing but just went on smiling his golden smile. Jess realised that she was enjoying the cleaning up more than the party.

'Who wants a hot chocolate?' she asked. 'I think we're due a break.'

'Oh no, don't dirty those mugs again!' said Flora. 'Ben's just washed and dried them . . . Oh, all right, you've convinced me!'

There was the sound of Jess's dad's footsteps coming downstairs. He entered the kitchen, looking a bit tired but not actively hostile.

'I've sorted out all Mum's papers,' he said. 'Nobody must touch anything in that room, though the carpet could do with some cleaning.'

'I'll vacuum it!' Ben Jones nodded. 'It's on my, uh, to do list.'

'And I'll shampoo it!' added Fred. 'I'm becoming addicted to carpet shampooing. I'm going to offer to shampoo the pitch at Manchester United.'

'I'm thinking of going now, Jess,' said Dad, yawning. 'This has been a long day. I've been up since five.'

'Oh, Dad, I forgot! Thanks so much for helping!'

'I just texted Mum,' Dad announced, putting on his jacket, 'and she's planning to arrive back mid-afternoon tomorrow. She says she and Granny will stop some-where for Sunday lunch. I didn't mention what happened here this evening. I didn't want to stress her out. You'll have to tell her when she arrives.'

'Mid-afternoon,' mused Jess. 'That gives us plenty of time.'

'I'll be here with you if you like,' said Dad kindly. 'I know this wasn't totally your fault. In fact, I feel a bit guilty about it myself.'

'Guilty? Why?'

He shrugged. 'I guess I feel guilty about everything, given the chance.' He smiled sadly. 'I feel really guilty about climate change.'

'Yes, that was really careless of you, Dad!' Jess gave him a big hug. 'You should have noticed you were single-handedly causing climate change and sorted it out years ago! But thanks so much for being so brilliant about this!'

Dad disentangled himself from the hug and zipped up his jacket (it was a rather stylish aviator jacket, a present from Phil).

'I'll be off, then,' he said. 'You'll be OK here, I presume?' He looked blearily round the group.

'Of course!' said Jess. She was so glad Dad hadn't asked her to go back to his flat with him. She was feeling better and better as the evening wore on. It was therapeutic cleaning and tidying her dear old home.

'I'll come by tomorrow morning, then,' said Dad. 'I might have a lie-in, though – I'll turn up about eleven, probably.'

'Fine!' said Jess, privately aware that if she got her way, she'd still be fast asleep at eleven.

Dad trudged off into the night, leaving Jess and co to sip their hot choc in the kitchen and chat about nothing in particular.

'Well,' said Fred eventually, 'I think I'll go up and shampoo the study carpet. I can't resist any longer!'

'Wait!' said Ben, picking up the vacuum cleaner. 'I have to vacuum it first.'

Jess put clean sheets on Granny's bed, then she and Flora finished off the kitchen.

'Well, I ought to be going,' Flora said, looking at her watch. 'My dad's been in a bit of a strop today and he said I've got to be home tonight.'

At this point there was the clattering sound of Ben carrying the vacuum cleaner downstairs. Flora went out into the hall, putting on her coat.

'Bye, Ben,' said Flora. 'I'm off now.'

'I should go, too,' said Ben, stashing the vacuum back in its place under the stairs. 'I'll walk you home if you like.'

It was getting late. Jess could hear the sounds of Fred working in her mum's study upstairs.

'Say bye to Fred for me,' said Flora as she kissed Jess goodbye. And she gave Jess an odd little look, the sort of look that couldn't be translated into words.

Jess felt a strange prickling all over her skin as she

realised that she and Fred were about to be home alone together.

'I'll give you a call tomorrow and I'll come over for some more lovely, lovely cleaning!' Flora smiled.

'I'll come, too,' promised Ben.

Jess thanked them again and, as she closed the door behind them, her heart missed a beat. She sensed that something extraordinary was going to happen.

Chapter 18

Jess hesitated in the hall. She felt suddenly shy. Who'd have thought that she'd find herself in this situation? She'd hardly seen Fred on his own for the past few weeks, because Jodie had been so relentlessly by his side. The one time they'd been alone together they'd had a punch-up. Now, unexpectedly, they had space and time . . . for what? For anything.

On the other hand, since Flora and Ben had gone, Fred might decide to go, too. If he did, she wouldn't try to stop him. Should she go upstairs to him now? Should she stay down here? In an instant the simplest things, that would be completely straightforward with anybody else, became weird ordeals and challenges. Jess loitered in the hall for a moment. The whole house was awfully quiet, apart from the faint scuffling sounds of Fred shampooing the carpet upstairs.

Jess went into the sitting room and examined her music collection. She chose a cheerful jazz number and turned it down to a moderate level so Mr Appleton next door wouldn't hear it and complain. The infectious rhythms of Dixieland were soon flooding out.

Jess relaxed a bit and looked around the room. There were dirty marks all over the window sill and the coffee table. She went to the kitchen to get a bucket of soapy water and a sponge. Fred was still upstairs. Jess decided she would go up after she'd cleaned the surfaces in here, if Fred hadn't come down before then.

Jess scrubbed the coffee table and window sill, then dried them, then buffed them into a divine shine with some of Granny's favourite beeswax polish. She noticed the bookcase was a bit dusty, so she polished that as well. She began to feel she wasn't just cleaning up after the party – she was also cleaning up after the last six weeks of normal family life. Mum surely wouldn't have the cheek to complain about the party if her whole house was getting a makeover!

And still Fred hadn't come downstairs. Jess flicked her duster over the sofa – a totally pointless act – and sat down for a minute. She glanced up at the wall clock. It was eleven thirty, heading for midnight. And still Fred hadn't come downstairs. Would Fred *ever* come downstairs? The room smelled nice, like a hotel or something. Jess wondered about the bees who had made the wax which had gone into the beeswax polish. It's the kind of thing that happens in your mind when you're trying very hard indeed not to think of something in particular.

Jess picked restlessly at the arm of the sofa. She thought about poor Jodie confined to her sofa for the next few days. She wondered whether Fred was planning to go and see her tomorrow. Surely he would! Well, Jess was going to go, anyway.

She heard a door open upstairs, and footsteps coming down. Her heart beat faster. She couldn't decide whether to get up off the sofa or stay where she was. But if she got up she'd have to strike an attitude or stage some kind of activity. She couldn't just stand there with her knees knocking. So she might as well stay sitting down.

Fred's face appeared around the edge of the door. Jess's heart gave a familiar frenzied leap.

'Slacking again, I see,' observed Fred. 'While I wrestle upstairs with your mother's carpet, removing stains that had been there for twenty years at least, you're swanning around down here. It's all right for some.'

'I wasn't swanning around, you idiot!' retorted Jess. 'I've just scrubbed and polished every surface in this entire room!'

There was a moment's pause, during which it became deafeningly obvious that they were alone in the house.

'So.' Fred spoke unusually loudly. 'Where is everybody?' He blushed slightly.

'They've gone home,' said Jess, blushing now herself. 'Flora said to say goodbye – she's coming back tomorrow.'

Fred and Jess both tried to look as if they were thinking about Flora coming back tomorrow. Desperate to break up the strange frozen atmosphere, Jess leapt up off the sofa – so suddenly it made Fred jump.

'I thought you were going to attack me then,' he remarked. 'Murder me or something, with a tin of polish and a duster. After all, you've got a history of violent assault where I'm concerned.'

'That wasn't a violent assault,' replied Jess with a smile. 'That was a fair fight! So . . . how about a coffee?' She was desperate to detain him and yet didn't want to say so. Now, right now, would be the awful moment when Fred would say, '*Thanks, but I'd better be going as well.*'

'A coffee? Yeah, why not?' said Fred.

Jess's heart frolicked joyfully, like a puppy on a sunlit lawn. He wasn't going yet! He wanted to stay a bit longer!

She dodged past him and went out to the kitchen. She didn't want to brush against him accidentally. She didn't want to give him the wrong idea. Or the right idea. Which was it? Her mind was reeling. She was totally confused. Jess put the kettle on.

'I'll have sugar in it as well,' said Fred rebelliously. 'I haven't been allowed to take sugar recently.'

'Jodie?' Jess stared challengingly at him. So it had been said. The J-word. 'I wonder how she is.'

There was a brief silence.

At this point the kettle started to make its seething, coming-to-the-boil noise which, happily, ended the awkward silence. When the coffee was made, Jess and Fred would have to find words to say to each other, words which somehow had to be ordinary and not dangerous, for at least the amount of time it takes to drink a mug of coffee. There was just one problem: how to make a coffee break last for ever?

Chapter 19

'So . . .'

They sat down in the kitchen on either side of the old pine table, which, having been scrubbed recently by Flora, had an unusually clean appearance.

Jess's mind went blank. She'd managed to say, 'So . . .' But now what?

Fred stared into his coffee as if he was a fortune teller gazing into his crystal ball for all the answers.

'The worst thing about this whole nightmare,' Jess rabbited on, desperate to keep talking, 'is that somebody nicked my bear.'

'Rasputin?!' exclaimed Fred indignantly. 'Sorry, that sounded like a sneeze. Rasputin? Surely not!'

'Whizzer was in my room with some of his chavvy chums,' Jess reported sadly. 'There was a girl there – I don't even know her name – and she was cuddling Rasputin. I bet she's abducted him.'

'If she has, I expect they'll send a ransom note,' suggested Fred. 'But even if they don't, Whizzer's bound to know who she is. We can go round to her house and demand to have him back.'

Fred looked self-conscious for a moment – probably, thought Jess, because of the phrase 'we can go round to her house', an innocent enough phrase, but somehow significant and strange in this situation. It pitched them straight back to the old days when they did everything together.

'I can't bear being without my bear,' Jess sighed.

'It's unbearable,' agreed Fred.

Another huge silence engulfed them. Though the silence was vast and deeply embarrassing, it was also, somehow, voluptuous, as if they were swimming in a thick, delicious smoothie. Just being with Fred felt like such a huge treat. He was looking at the table, tracing the whorls of woodgrain with his finger. Jess realised she had missed seeing his long, knobbly fingers.

'Don't worry, we'll get him back,' said Fred. 'The important thing is not to get the police involved. Kidnappers always hate that.' He looked up with a small, shy smile.

'I wouldn't want to get the police involved,' she replied. 'With my record of previous convictions, I wouldn't stand a chance.' She was trying hard to get into comedy mode, but it was oddly difficult.

'Yes,' commented Fred. 'The first three murders you did were very stylish, but that last one with the peanut butter was frankly gross and I don't blame the police for coming down hard on you.'

Jess felt compelled to be serious again for a moment. 'To be honest, this evening I thought somebody might call the police for real. One of the neighbours, I mean.'

'Luke's dad?' asked Fred. 'Oh, he was going to, but I talked him out of it.' He gave a cheeky grin. Fred was managing so much better than she was right now. Her heart was fluttering like a butterfly against a window-pane. She was sure Fred could see the throbbing in her neck.

'Mr Appleton was so *not* going to call the police, Fred, you idiot!' she laughed. 'He was just a bit concerned, that's all. I suppose as the nearest parental figure he felt responsible or something. He cheered up loads when he heard my dad was coming.'

'Did Luke come to the party?' asked Fred suddenly, staring straight at her.

He blushed again. She blushed in response. They were getting through a lot of blushing tonight. There would be a shortage of blood soon. They would get cold feet as the blood rushed constantly to their faces. *Well, I have got cold feet, actually*, thought Jess. Sitting talking to Fred like this was mysteriously terrifying.

She was tongue-tied and her brain was refusing to cooperate. She felt muddled and desperate, like a wildcat locked in a library. She assumed that, once the coffee was finished, Fred would have to leave. Before then, she just had to make the most of this opportunity and say something – anything – that at least sounded normal. To be witty and delightful, let alone marvellous, was clearly beyond her at present.

'Luke?' she pondered. 'I think he's in Manchester this weekend. He goes up most weekends to visit his girlfriend.'

There was a silence.

'I didn't really like him at first,' said Fred thoughtfully. 'It was a combination of his film-star looks and his heroic work in Africa plus his Oscar and his Nobel prize – I felt he was trying just a bit too hard for a guy who's still under twenty.'

'Don't forget his Grammys and Emmys,' added Jess.

'Legendary,' agreed Fred. 'And don't you forget his Olympic Gold Medal for Posing and Smiling.'

'That's not fair!' laughed Jess. 'Luke's not a poser. He's a really genuine guy. He can't help being perfect.'

'Oh well,' said Fred, leaning back in his chair and looking across at Jess with a curious expression in his grey eyes; they seemed to cloud with mist and then clear to brightness, and then cloud over again, like April skies.

The CD had ended and the house seemed strangely eerie. The sitting-room clock struck three times to indicate it was a quarter to midnight.

'I'll put some more music on,' said Jess. 'Any requests?'

'Got any calypso?' asked Fred.

'No chance!' Jess laughed. 'Our music collection is so last century. The most recent item is Granny's Sinatra archive.'

'Sinatra is great!' Fred looked pleased. 'Let's have Sinatra.'

They went into the sitting room, which had an odd, expectant look, partly because it was uncharacteristically clean and tidy, and partly because the lateness of the hour somehow seemed to be seeping through the windows and creating an atmosphere of deep midnight strangeness.

'It's strange, having the house so tidy,' she commented, getting out a couple of coasters to protect the coffee table before setting her mug down. 'It's so different from the way things usually are. Granny's the only person in our house who's anywhere near tidy.'

'Perhaps your mum will be furious to find the house so clean,' suggested Fred, flinging himself down on the sofa.

Jess put on a Sinatra CD and selected the armchair. She didn't want to join Fred on the sofa. It would be too close. Besides, the way he had flung himself down, full length, made it difficult for anyone to join him. Had he done that on purpose? Had he deliberately made it impossible for Jess to sit near him? On the other hand, that was the way with Fred and sofas – he tended to dive on to them. His motto was always *Why stand if you can sit, and why sit if you can lie?*

'Take your shoes off!' commanded Jess.

'No need to shout!' Fred sat up and unlaced his trainers. 'I was just going to.'

'It's just that everywhere is so immaculate,' explained Jess. 'If the house was a tip as normal, I wouldn't mind shoes on the sofa. I wouldn't mind shoes on the ceiling!'

'Well, that's a big mistake on your part.' Fred rebuked her with a smile. 'I've always thought you're a bit of a barbarian when it comes to etiquette.'

'You're the barbarian!' laughed Jess.

Fred unlaced his other trainer and then paused. 'We have a problem,' he said slightly awkwardly. 'I know my feet are going to stink to high heaven. You have to prepare yourself.'

'Oh yes, your feet!' exclaimed Jess. 'I'd forgotten.'

They both blushed again at this accidental reference to their happier past – a time, quite recently, when Jess had had access to the delightful fragrance of Fred's feet whenever she'd wanted.

Fred sat thoughtfully on the sofa with his trainers unlaced. 'The problem is,' he confessed, 'I haven't got any of those charcoal-infused designer insoles. So my feet basically smell like feet, and I have to admit these are the same socks I was wearing this afternoon when I was out running.'

'Don't worry,' said Jess. 'I'll just scream a few times and gasp for breath and rush out of the room, but don't take it personally.'

'Well, I think I'll go upstairs and wash my feet,' said Fred, heading for the door, where he stopped. 'You can come with me if you like.'

'Wow! What an invitation!' enthused Jess. 'How could I possibly refuse?'

They went upstairs to the bathroom. Down in the sitting room, Frank Sinatra was crooning delightfully. The house felt more relaxed with music playing, but Jess was still on edge.

She entered the bathroom first and sat down on the little stool. Fred sat on the edge of the bath. It felt even more odd being together in the bathroom of all places, the most private room in the house.

'Brace yourself,' said Fred.

Chapter 20

Jess buried her face in a towel, and Fred took off his shoes and socks, swung one long leg up to the washbasin and started washing his foot. Gingerly Jess emerged from her towel. She could hardly smell Fred's feet at all. She picked up his discarded sock and sniffed it.

'This is totally unnecessary,' she remarked. 'Your sock is no worse than the average Cheddar with chives.'

'Usually it's Gorgonzola with a hint of chemical catastrophe,' said Fred, finishing off his first foot.

Jess reached for the towel which was flung over the radiator. It was disappointingly cold. 'Oh no! The heating has gone off,' she said. It was nearly midnight, of course. 'I'll go and switch it on again,' she said. The house had to be warm! She didn't want to drive Fred away, shivering, as the temperature plummeted and the house became the Ice Queen's Palace.

Jess ran downstairs, her mind racing. How much longer was Fred going to stay? Did his parents know where he was? (She'd inherited that kind of thinking from her mum.) Did he still have feelings for her or not? (She'd inherited that sort of thinking from her dad.) Was it possible that there was a murderer stalking around the garden who would break in and massacre them? (That was Granny's contribution.)

What was going on in Fred's head? (At last, a thought of Jess's very own!) Was he planning to leave? The foot-washing didn't fit into that kind of scenario. No one ever sighs wearily and says, '*It's late and I've got to be going, but first, do you mind if I just . . . wash my feet?*' Feet-washing showed a desire to please, surely. You wouldn't wash your feet if you were stuck with somebody you didn't like. If Jess was forced to spend time with the evil and disgusting Whizzer, for example, she would prepare by smearing Camembert and anchovies and dead squirrels all over her toes and then thrusting them in his face.

Fred had washed his feet because he didn't want to offend her. He was obviously planning to spend some more time lying on her sofa with his trainers off. Jess's heart gave an excited little flip as she switched the central heating back on. Seconds later she noticed something which set her thinking. It was a box of matches by the cooker.

There was an open fireplace in the sitting room, and on special occasions Mum and Granny would light a fire. Christmas, for example, New Year's Eve, birthdays, or during a cold snap. Jess had a sudden overwhelming urge to light a fire. She knew there were still some dry logs out in the garden shed and a few old wooden crates which Mum used for kindling. The newspapers were out there, too. She had a quick look in the cupboard under the sink – firelighters!

By the time Fred came downstairs again, she was kneeling by the fireplace, building a little pyramid of kindling and placing a few dry logs around it.

'What's going on?' asked Fred. 'Are we camping?'

'Defo!' replied Jess, striking the first match. 'I think it'll work OK because these logs feel nice and dry.'

'Wow, you're so outdoorsy all of a sudden!' exclaimed Fred. 'You're the chief scout of Ashcroft School.'

'Yes,' smiled Jess. 'I've had to learn survival techniques, having a mum who works as a librarian and is a useless cook. I can make a tasty meal out of a pair of old slippers. Your trainers, for example, slow cooked with wine and herbs, could feed a family of six for days.'

The fire was soon crackling brightly. Fred held out his hands to the blaze, kneeling beside her on the hearthrug. His hands were now so close to hers they were almost touching, but there was no sign he was thinking of making any kind of move. It wouldn't be right, anyway.

Jess withdrew to her chair and looked across at him. Even though they'd been such a famous team, such a legendary couple, such an apparently fixed constella-tion in the starry sky of lurve, somehow they were now doomed to occupy opposite sides of the hearthrug even if a romantic fire was blazing. Also, Jess knew she could never face Jodie tomorrow if something happened between her and Fred tonight.

'Got any candles?' asked Fred. 'I mean, the camping idea . . . candles would be nice. We could burn the house down. Destroy the evidence of the awful party.'

'Candles! Yes!' Jess raced to Granny's room, where she knew there was a secret stash in the bedside cabinet, in case of a power cut. She got three out and grabbed Granny's classy silver candelabra.

Soon the candles were glowing in the soft air of the sitting room, the fire was crackling, and outside in the dark an owl was faintly hooting.

'There goes your familiar, the owl,' said Jess, remembering a day when she and Jodie and Flora had designated an animal familiar to every boy they knew.

'Well, I am famously wise, of course,' said Fred. 'And occasionally I do tear rats' heads off if I get hungry in the middle of the night, but apart from that, I think I'm a bit more like a slug, to be honest.'

'Yes, naturally – a slug!' Jess nodded. 'What animal do you think I was in a previous existence?'

Fred looked at her thoughtfully. He was still sitting kind of curled up on the hearthrug, warming his hands. 'Possibly a killer whale,' he suggested. 'Or, in your better moods, a red panda.'

Jess wasn't about to waste time wondering if this was a coded message for *I still lurve you*. It so clearly wasn't. She stared instead at the fire, which was getting going nicely.

'I'd rather watch a fire than almost anything on TV,' she commented.

'Yeah,' agreed Fred. 'Though I do prefer fires which don't have ads in the middle.'

'Do you ever have an open fire at home?' asked Jess, her voice seeming strangely formal somehow.

'You sounded a bit like the Queen just then,' said Fred. 'No, we don't have fires, ma'am. We don't even have the central heating on much at this time of year. My dad is so mean. He's always trying to save money.'

'He's not an ogre like Flora's dad, though, is he?' mused Jess.

Fred's dad was a mysterious man who had spent some time in the army, and as a result was unexpectedly good at such things as doing the ironing and running a bar. Jess felt the conversation drying up and she began to be anxious. How were they ever going to keep talking, with so much that they ought not to say?

She switched back into Queenie mode. 'Have you come far?' she enquired in a high, royal voice.

'It's not how far I've come,' said Fred, looking right into her eyes in a disconcerting way. 'It's where I'm going.'

Jess's heart missed a beat. 'And where is that?' she enquired frostily and regally.

'Frankly,' said Fred, shrugging, 'I haven't got the faintest idea. But in the short-term, I'm heading for that sofa.' He scrambled up and took a flying leap, crashing down on to the sofa like a tree that has been felled.

Jess felt an excited thrill run through her veins. Fred was definitely going nowhere soon . . .

Chapter 21

Now what Jess most wanted was to turn the lights off so it would be just firelight and candlelight. But how could she do that without it seeming, well, needy, predatory and inappropriately romantic?

'Turn that top light off, Queenie, there's a good maj,' said Fred, effortlessly solving her problem. 'It's hurting my eyes.' He covered his eyes with his hand.

Jess bounded to the light switch. Now a glamorous duskiness spread through the room. She returned to her chair. The fire crackled cosily. The candles quivered in a faint breath of air. Fred turned over on his side and stared at the fire.

'I apologise in advance,' he yawned, 'for the fact that I might just drop off to sleep.'

Jess was slightly hurt by this remark, and the yawn.

She had never felt less sleepy in her life. Her heart was thudding and every nerve in her body was dancing with electricity because she and Fred were alone together, with hours and hours stretching away ahead of them, and nobody to interrupt or intrude on them. And he felt *sleepy*!? Boys were so totally clueless – unless he was just pretending to feel sleepy. It was, after all, quite an atmospheric scenario. Maybe Fred wanted to downplay the romantic overtones.

'So.' Jess was determined to try and arrive at some kind of understanding. They might never get another chance like this. She was tormented by the sense that things had gone horribly wrong between them and, even if she would never be able to put them right, she did at least want to be able to talk to him properly and find out what he was really feeling.

She was terribly tempted to ask, '*How are things with Jodie?*', but she had the feeling that if she said that the evening would be ruined. Fred would prob-ably jump up like a scalded cat and run off howling into the night. She had to find out what he was think-ing, but subtly, cleverly. Jess's mind whirled, but drew a blank. Then, out of desperation, she said, 'With you flat out on the couch like that, it's like I'm your psychiatrist and you're my patient. What's your earliest memory?'

Fred looked startled but obviously decided to play along. 'My earliest memory . . .' he pondered. 'It's got to be when I was sick all over Helen Gomberts at play-group. It was my finest moment. It's been downhill all the way since then.'

'Downhill? How exactly?' asked Jess in an American psychoanalyst's voice.

There was such a long silence that Jess was afraid Fred was drifting off to sleep because he was lying on his back now, with his eyes closed. But eventually he turned over on to his side again and stared into the fire.

'Everything's gone haywire,' he murmured with a sigh. He didn't sound as if he was kidding. 'I don't recognise myself in the mirror any more.'

'What do you mean?' breathed Jess. Was he about to confess that he felt wrong with Jodie?

'Sometimes,' he went on hesitantly, 'I seem to be a giraffe, sometimes a duck-billed platypus.' Ah! He was still kidding.

'What are you really?' asked Jess in a whisper.

'If I really was an owl in a previous existence,' he mused, 'maybe that's why I feel as if I've eaten a poisoned rat.'

'Do you feel as if you've eaten a poisoned rat?' enquired Jess tremulously. As a definition of a relationship crisis it certainly had a lot of power.

There was another pause, during which Fred just stared at the fire. Jess held her breath. Eventually she decided she had to say something. Boys were so useless when they tried to talk about feelings.

'So,' she suggested gently, 'let's think about this. If you could go back in time, how far would you go?'

'The thirteenth of February,' said Fred instantly.

The day before Valentine's Day, when she had dumped him! Jess's heart leapt.

'No, wait – I was being a spineless twit long before that,' he went on, glaring angrily at the fire. 'Say, mid-January. We've got to take it back to before that nightmare in Dorset.'

Jess's heart was galloping now. She and Fred had gone to stay with Flora's ex-boyfriend's family in their house by the sea in Dorset, where Fred had somehow been made to feel like an outsider and had reacted stupidly by sulking and disappearing. He went back home early without saying a word to anybody. Jess had been left feeling embarrassed because he was supposed to be her boyfriend for goodness' sake, and she hadn't had the faintest idea what was going on, or even where he was.

'I suppose the further back I go, the more evidence I find that I'm totally spineless,' said Fred.

Jess hesitated. She was so, so tempted to hurl herself at the sofa, fall into Fred's arms and cry, '*You may be spineless, but you're* **my** *spineless twit and I lurve you more than words can say!*' But fortunately she did have a shred of pride left.

The fact remained that Fred was with Jodie now, at least in some sense, though why he was lying here on her sofa at gone midnight in the firelight and candle-light was something of a tantalising mystery.

At this point Fred's phone rang. He sat up, fished it out of his pocket and stared at the caller ID on the screen. Then he sort of tossed it away on to the hearth-rug as if it was too hot to handle. Jess could clearly see that it was *Jodie* calling.

'Answer it!' she hissed. It seemed wrong to ignore it.

Fred gave her an anxious panicky glance, picked up the phone and answered the call. 'Hi,' he said, and Jess could tell that he was trying to sound sleepy.

She got up swiftly and left the room. Of course she was going to eavesdrop, but she didn't want to eaves-drop right under his nose, bold as brass. She was going to creep out to the kitchen and eavesdrop from there.

Chapter 22

Jess lurked in the kitchen with her ears flapping. She had terrific hearing and could often hear what people were saying in Australia, so to eavesdrop on Fred now was a cinch.

'Well, I was asleep,' he said. *Lie number one*, thought Jess.

'Of course I am! Where else would I be?' *Lie number two*. Jess couldn't help feeling satisfied that he was lying, but she was also guilty and uneasy.

'Oh, bad luck. Have you taken any painkillers?' Presumably Jodie was having trouble sleeping and her leg was hurting. Jess felt a twinge of anxiety and concern.

'Oh yeah?' Hmm, what did he mean by that? That reply stayed a mystery.

'Yes, yes . . . I know.' Jodie could go on a bit, and clearly she wasn't in the mood to sleep right now.

'Of course I will . . . That might be a bit early . . . For goodness' sake, woman! It's the weekend . . . OK, then. OK . . . OK . . . I know . . .'

Jess began to feel embarrassed about listening, partly because Fred seemed to be deliberately not giving anything away – as if he knew she was listening. And though she was listening, she didn't want him to assume she was listening. And anyway, he obviously wasn't going to say anything of interest. So, acting on impulse, she opened the back door and walked out into the garden.

Light spilled out from the kitchen window, and Jess's heart lurched once again at the sight of Mum's beloved daffodils, lying all crushed and wretched where the gatecrashers had fallen on them. She'd managed, with the help of Dad and her brilliant friends, to clear up the house, but what can you do about a whole swathe of daffodils that are ruined and were the pride and joy of their owner?

Jess knew how much her mum would be looking forward to being reunited with her garden – her daughter came a very poor second in her affections. It was going to be awful tomorrow – no, wait! It had gone midnight so Mum would be back later *today*! She heaved an exasperated sigh, and then suddenly Fred appeared at her side.

'Look at this.' She shrugged hopelessly. 'You know what my mum's like about her garden and the daffs were like her favourite children.'

'You could always just cut them all off and tell her somebody came in the night and stole them,' he suggested.

'Don't be silly, Fred! That would be worse!'

There was a silence while they stared at the trashed garden. An owl hooted nearby.

'Woodsmoke,' said Fred, sniffing the air. 'That's from our fire.'

'Let's get back to it.' Jess wanted to escape from the trashed garden.

They went indoors and knelt on the hearthrug again. The fire was building up heat and Fred put another log on the blaze. They stared at the flames for a while in silence.

'So how was Jodie?' asked Jess boldly. It was stupid to pretend she hadn't known it was Jodie. It was obvious.

'She can't sleep,' said Fred. 'Keeps getting twinges in her leg. She's bored.'

'Jodie's often bored,' commented Jess. She wondered if Jodie would ever get bored with Fred and, if so, how soon she could conveniently manage it.

Fred made no remark on the subject of Jodie's low boredom threshold.

'I'll definitely go and see her tomorrow,' said Jess. 'When will you be there?'

Fred looked a bit edgy and threw her a sideways glance. 'I'm not sure.' He hesitated.

'I expect she'll be in a bad mood,' said Jess. Then, in case that sounded a bit harsh, she added, 'I know I would be. But I expect you'll cheer her up.' She tried hard not to make this sound jealous or bitter.

'That does seem to be my role in life at the moment,' murmured Fred. 'She certainly needs a lot of cheering up. Did you know her dad is ill?'

This question soared into Jess's brain like a strange dangerous rocket. 'Ill? No! What's the matter with him?' asked Jess anxiously.

'Not sure, but he's having chemo,' said Fred, poking the fire in an absent-minded way.

Jess's heart sank. 'Oh no! That means cancer.'

Fred nodded and still stared at the fire.

'Oh, it's so awful! Is he going to get better?' asked Jess.

Fred shrugged. 'I hope so. He's a nice guy.'

'I'm amazed that Jodie never told anybody! Except you.'

'She didn't tell me,' explained Fred. 'Her dad did. We were watching a bit of football on TV while she was putting some make-up on or something. He just casually mentioned that he had cancer and said it was a good job he was bald already. He's a funny guy, actually.'

Jess was silent for a minute, thinking of the unimaginable awfulness if it had been her dad who was undergoing treatment with his survival not certain.

'It's so awful! I just wish she'd told us.'

'But, then, if she did tell everybody . . .' Fred had obviously discussed this with Jodie, '. . . she'd have to put up with everybody saying, "Oh, how awful", and staring pityingly at her with puppy-dog eyes. Could you bear that?'

'It would be horrible,' Jess agreed.

For a moment she stopped thinking about Jodie's dad being ill and considered the fact that Fred and Jodie had had this serious conversation which she, Jess, knew nothing about. Over the weeks they must have had dozens and dozens of private conversations; Fred and Jodie talking, and it was none of her business.

So far, when she'd thought about them being

together, it was the kissing that she'd been focusing on, imagining it in ghastly tormenting detail. Now she realised they'd also been talking all this time, and that the talking was, somehow, almost worse.

'I must go and cheer her up tomorrow, too,' said Jess. 'Poor Jodie!'

'Yes,' said Fred simply. 'She'd like that. She's really gutted about not being able to do the half-marathon, because of course she was running in aid of Cancer Research. We were doing it in aid of the earthquake victims, but when her dad got his diagnosis she changed her mind.'

'Oh, so Jodie wanted to raise money for her dad's charity!'

Fred nodded sadly. Since he so often acted as if Jodie was a nuisance and a bossyboots, it was odd to hear him saying things that were respectful and not unkind and jokey. Jess hoped fervently that he would say something unkind and jokey soon, though, even if it was directed at her. Fred being solemn was a strange experience, but she was glad that he was capable of it. Wisecracking isn't always appropriate.

This was the moment to say something really direct, really important, which she couldn't possibly have said earlier, when they'd been kidding around.

'I've been having trouble getting my head around this Jodie business,' she confessed, staring into the fire. 'But now, well, I hope you do manage to cheer her up and make her feel better. Good luck!'

For a moment Fred put his arm around her shoulders, but in a quiet, ceremonious kind of way that could not be interpreted as Making A Move.

'Got to do it,' he sighed. 'She's had bad luck.'

Jess felt the warmth of his arm all along her shoulders. Though seized with the hugest desire in the world to grab him and plant an adoring kiss on his lips, she controlled herself.

Fred gently removed his arm. 'Who knows what the future holds?' He sighed.

They needed to get back to safer ground, away from this quivering quicksand of terrible things that could not be said, before they got sucked down into it and did or said something they would regret.

'I like the new compassionate Fred Parsons,' said Jess, trying to ease the conversation back towards comedy, but with nothing too coarse or tasteless.

'I quite like him myself,' said Fred. 'I didn't think I had it in me, but I may have a future tiptoeing around hospitals.'

'You'd probably trip over somebody's drip and

send them spiralling into a coma,' suggested Jess, smiling. 'But, even though I'm impressed by your new saintliness, I'm not going to let you hog the sofa this time!' She sprang up and hurled herself on to it. 'And don't you dare fight me for it or I'll give you another black eye!'

'I'm quite happy on the hearthrug,' said Fred, stretching out beside the fire. 'In fact, I think I may have been a smelly old dog in a previous existence.'

'Previous?' laughed Jess. 'You're a smelly old dog now!'

'True,' sighed Fred. 'And thank you for not mentioning it.'

They lay for a while in the firelight, almost side by side, Jess up on the sofa, Fred below on the hearthrug, staring into each other's eyes.

'My eyes are starting to itch,' said Jess. 'I think it's the heat of the fire. I'm getting a bit sleepy.'

'I'm not sleepy at all,' boasted Fred, his grey eyes seeming to get bigger and bigger, until Jess felt she could dive into them. 'First one to go to sleep is a nincompoop!'

'We both know perfectly well that you're the nincompoop,' said Jess sternly. 'You were born a nincompoop and you will die a nincompoop's death.'

'Yes,' admitted Fred. 'And it'll probably involve some kind of small furry animal. I have a feeling I may be nibbled to death by bushbabies.'

'I certainly hope so.' Jess smiled. 'And I hope to be there to see it.'

There was a trembling pause.

'You will be,' said Fred quietly.

Those three little words offered Jess more comfort and solace than she had imagined possible in their present situation. Now she understood why she was more jealous of Jodie and Fred's talking than their kissing. What made Fred so extraordinary was what went on in his mind.

Still staring at Fred's grey eyes, Jess let herself feel drowsy. Her eyelids became heavy and drooped. She forced them open a couple of times and found Fred was still staring at her. Smiling, she drifted off to sleep.

Jess awoke with a sudden shrill ringing in her ears. For an instant she didn't know where she was. Then she remembered, and the memory was delicious.

Daylight flooded the sitting room, but where was

Fred? The hearthrug was empty. A cosy mohair throw was snuggled over her – how odd, she couldn't remember pulling that over herself.

There was the ringing again. Oh no! It was the doorbell!

Jess sprang off the sofa. For a terrible moment she thought it was Mum and Granny come back already, but then she remembered that Dad had said he was going to drop over in the morning to assess the situation. She glanced at her watch while stumbling to let him in – it was indeed eleven o'clock. She opened the front door and stared out blearily at Dad, who looked tidy and well dressed as usual.

'You've just woken up,' said Dad accusingly. 'And I bet you stayed up half the night, gassing to your mates.'

'No, no!' insisted Jess.

She realised that Dad must not know that Fred had stayed last night. If indeed Fred had. She had no idea when he had left. She had no idea even *if* he had. Jess had a sudden horrid feeling that Fred might be upstairs in the bathroom. At any moment he could appear on the landing, posing cheekily in boxer shorts. That would be a disaster.

'I've been up for hours!' she lied.

'Oh yeah?' Dad smiled sceptically as he stepped

inside. 'You must think I was born yesterday. You've got crumply marks all over your cheek.'

Jess felt flustered. She knew that more lies would be necessary, but the trouble was, she wasn't at all sure what those lies should be. So she just kissed her dad on the cheek and kept her fingers crossed.

Chapter 23

'So, shall we take a tour of the house?' asked Dad.

They trudged upstairs. Jess was on edge. She still wasn't convinced that Fred had gone and, as she threw open the door to her own room, she had a horrible nightmarish dread that Fred would be sprawled on her bed, sipping champagne. But there was nobody there, not even Rasputin (and the thought of his absence made her feel sick all over again).

'Hmmm,' said Dad. 'OK, let's see Mum's study.'

He was obviously going to be fixated on Mum's study because of all his work laundering her papers. They stood in the doorway and surveyed the scene. Everything was stacked neatly: box files, papers, books. In fact, it was tidier than it had ever been before. The carpet looked wonderfully clean and fluffy.

'Fred made a good job of the carpet, didn't he?' she commented.

Dad nodded, though he was still gazing rapturously at his own handiwork.

'And it was brilliant of you to iron the papers and stuff,' Jess added hastily.

Dad sighed in a satisfied way. 'I wish she'd paint this room white,' he said. 'This mossy green look is so dated. Plus it makes the room feel dark.'

'I hope you haven't finished painting your bathroom yet!' cried Jess, remembering. 'Did you do some this morning?'

'No,' said Dad. 'I had a lie-in. Don't worry, the hideous orange is still there, waiting for you to obliterate it.'

Next they examined Mum's little bedroom, which was tidy and smelled fresh, and the bathroom, which was sparkling.

'The place looks a lot better than normal,' commented Jess. 'Maybe I should host a rave every month just for the sake of the clean-up afterwards.'

'You were very, very lucky that no serious damage was done,' said Dad as they went downstairs. 'Thank goodness we nipped the party in the bud before things got too wild and messy.'

'Granny's photo frame was damaged,' admitted Jess as they looked into Granny's room. 'It just needs a new bit of glass. I can get it tomorrow after school with my pocket money.'

'Or just get a whole new frame,' suggested Dad. 'It'll be easier than finding glass to fit the old one.'

'The worst damage,' she confessed as they walked into the kitchen, 'was to Mum's daffodils. You know she's got a big patch of them outside the back door, and how they're her pride and joy? Well, some people trampled on them last night and the whole bed is absolutely ruined.'

'Uh-oh!' groaned Dad. 'Now that is bad news. She'll go ballistic.'

'It's awful,' sighed Jess, unlocking the back door. 'Come and see.'

They went out into the sunlight, and Jess stopped in her tracks. A big, bright, shiny, golden swathe of daffodils stood where the smashed and ruined ones had been just hours earlier. Jess stared at them, speechless.

'They look perfectly OK,' said Dad. 'I don't know what you were worrying about. Maybe they perked up in the night.'

'No, no, no, Dad, these aren't the same daffs!' Jess

was flabbergasted. 'No way were those smashed ones going to perk up and look like this. The leaves were all bruised and torn, but . . . these leaves are perfect.' Jess was completely and utterly stunned. Her mother's pride and joy had been miraculously resurrected. But how? Who had done this?

'Oh, you'd be surprised at how flowers can perk up,' said Dad, who famously knew nothing about gardening (according to Mum). 'Either that, or your guardian angel's been at work.' He smiled playfully at Jess and took a brief look around.

The only sign that there had ever been a party was a group of six black plastic rubbish sacks lined up by the door in the fence at the bottom of the garden.

'I don't think Mum's going to be unduly cross,' he said. 'Right! Let's go back indoors and you can make me a cup of coffee. It's a bit chilly out here. You'd never think it was spring – I'm going to ask for my money back.'

'Yes! It was so cold last night that we lit a fire!' Jess told him as they nipped back indoors. Instantly she knew it had been a mistake to mention it.

Dad was surprised. 'A fire? When?' He looked sharply at her. 'What, in the sitting room?'

He went through to the sitting room and inspected

the hearth. The fireguard was placed across the front (Fred must have done that, too) and the only untidy thing was Jess's throw. She picked it up and folded it, feeling edgy.

'Yeah, we lit the fire when we'd more or less finished clearing up and just sat around it for a bit for a break,' she said, trying to sound casual but aware she was blushing again.

'You and who else?' asked Dad mischievously. 'I see you lit some candles, too. Romantic, was it? The big reunion between you and Fred?'

'No, no!' said Jess hastily.

Dad mustn't know what really happened, especially when she hardly knew herself. It had been a very strange episode, full of tantalising hints and a mysterious atmosphere, like something out of a fairy story. She hoped Fred wouldn't tell anyone. Above all, Jodie must not know. Actually nobody must know, not even Flora. Jess couldn't absolutely trust Flora not to gossip. It was her one major fault.

'It was just me and Flora,' Jess went on recklessly.

'Did she stay over?' asked Dad casually as they went back to the kitchen.

'No, she went home.' Jess walked over to the kettle and kept her back to Dad as she filled it. It was easier to lie to him if he couldn't see her face. 'Her dad's a bit of an ogre and he's going through a strict phase.'

'I must try one of those some day,' quipped Dad.

Jess laughed, grateful for the chance to change the subject. 'Too late, Daddo! You've already established your reputation as the biggest wuss in the world! You'd prefer decaf, I assume?'

'No! Give me coffee with caffeine in it! I must somehow pretend I'm a real man!'

'Dad! You know if you have caffeine you feel sick for hours and then you can't sleep! Just have your normal decaf or a nice cuppa tea, Granny-style!'

'Don't! Don't! These cruel taunts!'

Dad seemed to be in a frisky mood this morning. He was clearly relieved that the house looked clean and tidy. Jess assumed that he'd been scared Mum would blame him if the place had been totally trashed. Thank goodness Jess had managed to get him away from the awkward subject of Fred.

'So . . .' Dad sat down at the kitchen table and beamed at her in a friendly way. 'How did things go with Fred? Did you manage to grab him back from Jodie's horrible clutches? Tell me every single detail!'

Chapter 24

Jess's heart lurched. She hadn't managed to avoid the dreaded F-word after all.

'Fred? Oh no, it wasn't like that,' she sighed. 'Jodie . . . couldn't come last night.'

'Perfect!' commented Dad. 'Why didn't you pounce, then?'

'The thing is,' said Jess, choosing her words carefully so as to avoid mentioning Fred as much as possible, 'I heard last night that Jodie's dad is having chemotherapy, plus Jodie pulled a hamstring yesterday so she's had to give up the half-marathon and she was going to get sponsored for Cancer Research, so she's absolutely gutted. And of course she's going to be stuck at home for days on end before her leg starts to heal. It's not really the moment for any pouncing. I think she needs Fred more than I do at the moment.'

'Whew!' breathed Dad. 'You're being a bit saintly about all this, aren't you?'

'Not really,' said Jess. 'Anyone would do the same.' She placed Dad's coffee on the table and got the bread out. 'Dad, would you mind cutting two slices of bread? Sorry to be such a baby, but I find it really hard.' Jess was grateful for the chance to talk about something ordinary.

'Nobody can cut bread till they're thirty,' said Dad. 'I'll join you in a piece of toast, if I may. And some of that lovely home-made marmalade from the farmers' market.'

They enjoyed a little breakfast, and Jess managed to steer the conversation away from Fred and Jodie and back to Dad's bathroom. But, as she half-listened to Dad lecturing madly about the best shades of blue for a bathroom that faces south, in the corners of her mind she was still thinking about Fred. When would she see him again?

Suddenly her mobile rang. She grabbed it, her heart hammering, but it was only Flora.

'Hi, babe! How did it go last night?'

'Oh, fine, the house looks amazing this morning.'

'I meant how did it go with Fred?'

Jess hoped Dad couldn't hear Flora and she

crammed the phone even more closely against her head, hoping that her mum was wrong about mobiles frying one's brain. 'Oh, nothing special.' She tried to keep it light-hearted. 'Dad's come over to inspect the place now and I'm hoping he's going to give it five stars.'

'Ah, your dad's there! Does that mean you can't talk about what happened last night?'

Jess hesitated. She didn't want Flora to know anything about last night. The longed-for reunion hadn't taken place, anyway. On the other hand, what had happened was strange and inexplicable.

'Oh, there's nothing to say on that subject,' she swept on. 'Did you get home OK?'

'Obviously, or I wouldn't be phoning you now,' laughed Flora. 'It turns out my dad had gone to bed when I got in, so I could have stayed a bit longer at your place – probably even stayed over. But I didn't want to spoil your evening by hanging about like a pathetic gooseberry.'

Jess racked her brains for a response that would satisfy Flora but could still be safely overheard by Dad. It was very complicated, lying in two directions at once. 'I do love gooseberries,' she said madly, randomly. 'I can't wait for them to be in season so we can make a crumble. When I say *we*, of course I mean Granny – her crumbles are legendary. Dad, when are gooseberries in season?'

'July, I think,' Dad pondered. 'They're the first fruit of the summer. So it may be June. No, June's too early. July, I should think. Or possibly August.'

Jess had to escape from this madness. 'Listen, Flo, if you're ringing to offer more help of the tidying sort,' she said, 'I don't think there's any need. The house looks beautiful. Thanks so much for your help last night.'

'No worries,' replied Flora. 'What are you doing for the rest of the day?'

'Well, I've got to be here to grovel when my mum gets home, and then I'm going to see Jodie. Do you wanna come?' Having Flora there when she visited Jodie would definitely be useful.

'Sorry, I can't really,' Flora replied, sounding rather shifty. 'I've still got bits of homework to do, plus lots of other stuff – chores and things. I'll keep in touch, though. Give Jodie my love!'

Jess said goodbye and ended the call with relief. Now she only had to lie in one direction – towards Dad.

'Why did the subject of gooseberries come up?' he asked playfully.

'Oh, no reason. Flora was just eating a gooseberry yogurt, that's all.'

'Oh, is that all?' Dad laughed. 'I thought maybe Flora said she left early last night so that you could have some time alone with Fred – she didn't want to feel like a gooseberry.'

'Honestly, Dad,' sighed Jess irritably. 'What a preposterous idea!'

Dad was quite scarily psychic sometimes. But luckily he didn't realise he was.

'So!' Jess prepared a shiny, bright, subject-changing smile. 'How about going over to your place and painting the bathroom?'

The landline rang. Jess jumped up and grabbed it.

'Jess, it's me.' It was Mum. She sounded ratty.

'Mum! How's it going?' Jess felt guilty that she hadn't phoned Mum earlier to find out how they were.

'It's all been very, very stressful,' said Mum. 'We're not going to stop for lunch on the way home. We'll be back in half an hour. I'm feeling very, very fragile.'

Oh no! Mum was feeling fragile! After offering a few comforting words, Jess hung up and turned to her dad.

'Mum's feeling very, very fragile and she'll be home in half an hour,' reported Jess. 'It's been very stressful, apparently.'

'Right!' exclaimed Dad, scrambling to his feet. 'I'm outta here!'

It seemed Jess was going to have to deal with Mum's fragility on her own.

Moments after Dad had left, the landline rang again. Jess grabbed it, assuming it was Mum about to deliver some afterthought about buying milk or something. But it was Alison, Mum's colleague from the library.

'Is Madeleine there, please, Jess?' she asked.

'She'll be back in half an hour or so,' Jess informed her.

'Oh dear, it's just I've heard a really awful rumour,' sighed Alison. 'She's going to be terribly upset.'

'Has somebody died?' asked Jess nervously.

'No, no, nothing like that. The rumour is that the council is planning to close the library.'

'Oh no!' exclaimed Jess, even though she was relieved that the rumour was nothing to do with her wild party.

'Yes,' said Alison grimly. 'Looks like we'll all be unemployed in a few months' time. Madeleine's going to go through the roof when she hears about it.'

At least, thought Jess nervously, *we do still have a roof for her to go through*. It was some comfort.

Chapter 25

Jess had just half an hour to prepare for Mum's arrival. First she removed all the mascara from her cheeks – in fact, she removed all the make-up she'd been wearing for the past week. Mum liked to see her looking 'natural' – whatever that meant – even though she'd seen old photos of Mum and Dad both wearing that kohl eyeliner made fashionable by Cleopatra.

There was no need to clean the house – it was immaculate. Jess showered, even though she felt that she was untidying the house by doing so. Drying herself afterwards, she thought how, once you'd got your house immaculate, you never wanted to do anything ever again, but just sit there, frozen, like a dummy in a shop window. That was one reason why it was so much better to be untidy.

The hardest thing was planning her speech. The speech in which she broke the news that Mum's house had almost been trashed by a gang of uninvited strangers on Saturday night. The timing was crucial. Obviously, she mustn't spring it on Mum the moment she walked in the door. Mum had sounded really stressed out on the phone – describing herself as 'very, very fragile' was quite extreme, even by her self-pitying standards. Mum had a slight tendency to martyrdom, which Jess was always trying to dispel by reminding her of her blessings. Actually, that could be the way to go! *'You're feeling fragile? Your weekend was stressful? Never mind! Think positive – at least your house wasn't completely trashed by hordes of strangers who burst in here on Saturday night.'* No, that would never do.

And on top of Mum's pre-existing fragility was the bombshell that Alison couldn't wait to drop. Jess would have to tell Mum about *that* as soon as she arrived. *'Mum, you're gonna be sacked – just ask Alison – but, still, never mind! At least the house wasn't completely trashed by the hundreds of gatecrashers who invaded on Saturday night!'* No, that would never do, either.

It's always hard having to break dodgy news to somebody who's already reeling from other bad stuff. Jess would just have to be on her toes. She would have to be ultra-considerate and wait for the perfect moment. No, there wouldn't be a perfect moment. She would have to choose the least bad moment.

Jess dressed to please the older generation in a jumper knitted for her by Granny and a pair of trousers bought for her last year by Mum. The effect was dire: she looked like her own great-grandmother. Then she went downstairs and put the kettle on. They were going to need oceans of tea to get through this crisis. Jess felt her stomach tighten with dread.

Suddenly, she remembered Fred lying on the hearthrug last night and staring into her eyes. Somewhere out there on the edge of all the bad stuff, was something sublime to cherish.

Right on cue, she heard Mum's car draw up outside. Jess's heart started to beat faster, though not in the pleasant way it had bounded last night when Fred had stayed. It now lurched in rather an ominous way. Though tempted to exit through the back door and run for her life, Jess forced herself to the front door and opened it to welcome them.

Mum was striding up the path looking grouchy. 'Get the cases out of the car, Jess,' she said, without any touching reunion or kind words.

Wow! This certainly was a mega strop.

'Where's the paracetamol?' Mum muttered as she stormed past.

Oh dear. This was going to be a 'headache day'.

Granny was gamely bringing up the rear, dragging her little weekend case.

'Let me take that for you, Granny!' cried Jess. 'How was your weekend? How was Great-Aunt Jane?'

'Oh, it was awful, dear.' Granny shook her head, looking distressed. 'Jane was so confused. She hardly knew who we were at times. She was rambling . . . I'm totally exhausted. I'm going for a lie-down.'

Granny headed straight for her room, and Jess followed with the case. The photo of Grandpa was in its usual place on the bedside table. Maybe Granny wouldn't notice that the glass was missing.

'Shall I put the case here?' asked Jess, stashing it out of the way, behind the door.

'Anywhere, anywhere,' said Granny irritably, kicking off her shoes and sinking on to her bed. She closed her eyes.

'I'll get you a cup of tea,' said Jess, trying to offer some comfort.

'No thanks, dear,' said Granny – unexpectedly. She had never been known to refuse tea. 'I've had far too much tea today. I was desperate for a pee on the way home and we couldn't find a loo anywhere, so I had to pee behind a hedge.'

'Oh no!' said Jess. She knew she was going to have to fight hard for years to eradicate that image from her mind. It might even require expensive psychotherapy.

'Just leave me to have a little nap, dear,' murmured Granny, turning her back on Jess. 'I'll be all right in an hour or so.'

Jess obeyed and went out for Mum's case, then took the car keys out and locked the car. Back in the kitchen, Mum was making herself a Three Ginger Drink, her herbal favourite with extra grated ginger root. This was a sure sign of a major headache. She seemed to be ignoring Jess. She hadn't even noticed that the house was so clean! *What a waste of time that was*, thought Jess. *I should have left it trashed*. On the other hand, it was convenient that Mum was so oblivious to her surroundings.

'I'll take your case upstairs,' said Jess.

'Thanks, darling,' muttered Mum, sitting down at the kitchen table and opening a new pack of paracetamol. She only called Jess 'darling' when things were difficult.

Jess took the case upstairs and put it in Mum's supertidy room. As Mum was usually rather untidy in her private space, she was bound to notice that change. And her study, of course – she would see in a flash that somebody had been washing and ironing her paper- work and shampooing her carpet. Jess had toyed with the idea of passing off the spick and span house as the result of a bet with Flora. But washing and ironing Mum's paperwork? That was going a bit far.

When she got downstairs, Mum was eating a biscuit. This was also a bad sign. When she was feeling buoyant and confident, Mum never needed biscuits. And she'd torn this pack open like a hyena killing its prey; the wrapper lay in pieces all over the table and crumbs were scattered everywhere. She hadn't even used a plate! Jess had to stifle a pang of annoyance that Mum was already messing up her nice clean house.

'Granny told me Great-Aunt Jane wasn't in very good shape.'

'No.' Mum looked grim. 'It was a bit pointless really, going up there. I don't think she's going to make it, and even if she does, she'll need months of physio- therapy. I hope I never have a stroke like that. I hope I have a big one. I hope I'm dead before I hit the floor.' This wasn't exactly the sort of thing you want to hear your mother say.

Suddenly Jess's unscheduled party seemed like a

very small deal indeed. But there was still the mind-blowing matter of Alison's phone call. 'Uhh, Alison rang.'

'What on earth does she want now? The woman's a menace. Fuss, fuss, fuss, fuss, fuss, fuss!'

'She asked you to ring her.' Jess didn't dare reveal that she knew what the call was about.

'I'll see her tomorrow.' Mum was in a rebellious mood. She grabbed another biscuit and broke its back with one feral snap of her magnificent fangs.

'She said it was important.'

'Huh! Important! Her idea of something important is to point out that I've parked my car in the wrong bay.'

'Really, Mum,' she said softly. 'I think you should ring her.' Jess had a hunch that the closing of the library would be a better crisis for Mum to deal with than a very ill aunt. It was something she could turn into a campaign. Mum was an activist and loved marching and speeches and petitions and trying to change things. No amount of marching and speeches was going to resurrect Great-Aunt Jane.

Mum reached drearily for the phone, which Jess had placed conveniently on the table. She dialled Alison's number.

'Hi, Alison!' she began, all sweetness and light. 'Sorry I was out when you rang. How are things?' Then, of course, as she began to listen, her face got darker and her expression more and more concerned. Her eyes widened and whitened. 'No!' Her nostrils flared. 'No! They can't!' Her hand turned into a fist. 'No! I don't believe it!'

Jess tiptoed down to the far end of the kitchen and looked fondly at the mug which Fred had drunk his coffee out of the previous night. It was a yellow one with white spots. It would be a sacred mug now. She just hoped that her mum wouldn't get in a massive strop because of the library closing and start to hurl china about. It would be tragic if she smashed the mug that had touched Fred's lips. But Jess hoped that, if such a thing happened, she would be able to accept it as just an accident and not see it as an ominous symbol.

Mum completed her call and then immediately downed her ginger tea. She stood up, bristling with indignation. 'They're planning to close the library!' she announced, outraged. 'But we'll fight them every inch of the way! I have to spend some time in my office on the phone to people!' And she went upstairs.

Jess heard her study door slam. She waited for Mum to come out again, to reappear at the top of the stairs, looking puzzled, and demand, '*Who's been messing about with my papers?*' But no such thing happened. There was only the faint sound of Mum starting a phone conversation. Evidently she hadn't noticed all Dad's handiwork. When she eventually got round to noticing it, maybe that would be the moment to fess up about the party.

Suddenly Granny appeared in the doorway, looking slightly rumpled and also puzzled.

'Jess,' she asked, 'I'm afraid I'm going to have to ask you a rather embarrassing question.'

Chapter 26

'I was dusting it, Granny,' blustered Jess. 'I dropped it and the glass smashed. I'll get you a new one tomorrow.'

Granny looked puzzled. 'What are you talking about, dear?' she asked.

Oh no! Jess had messed up, big time. It hadn't been Grandpa's photo that Granny was concerned about.

'The photo of Grandpa – on your bedside table,' Jess blundered on. 'The glass smashed. I'm so sorry. I'll get you a brand new frame.'

'No, no. It's not that.' Granny shook her head as if a fly was buzzing around her. 'It's my envelope. Have you moved my envelope?'

'What envelope?'

'I keep an envelope in the drawer of my bedside table, and it's gone.'

'An envelope?' Jess was mystified. 'What sort of envelope?'

'It's got money in it,' said Granny. 'Over three hundred pounds. I'm saving up for my funeral expenses.'

Jess was horrified twice over. Firstly, that her dear little Granny was going to have a funeral one day. Secondly, at the revelation that her dear little funeral fund had been stolen by those gatecrashers who were in her room last night. Who were they? How dare they? How would Jess ever be able to repay her? And worst of all, judging by Granny's rather severe expression, she thought it was Jess who had been stealing from her!

'Granny!' she screamed in anguish. 'It wasn't me! Hand on heart I swear it wasn't me!'

'Well, who was it, then?' persisted Granny. 'Because it's gone.'

At this most awkward of moments the doorbell rang. Jess ran to answer it, and Granny followed. Mum also, unexpectedly, thundered down the stairs. There was a family reunion by the front door.

'This'll be Alison,' said Mum. 'She's coming over for a council of war. And so's Rob.' Rob was the junior librarian and Jess had always thought he was slightly attractive in a monkey-ish sort of way.

Mum opened the door. But it wasn't Alison or Rob. It was Mr Appleton from next door. He smiled his gentle, melancholy, peace-making smile.

'I just popped round to say,' he murmured reassuringly, 'that it wasn't as bad as all that on Saturday night, and Jess did brilliantly, and Jess's father was a hero, and there weren't *that* many of them, and I wasn't disturbed at all.'

The idiot! The idiot! Jess longed to rip his gentle, melancholy, peace-making smile right off his chops and strangle him with it.

'There weren't all that many what?' asked Mum, frowning.

Mr Appleton looked at Jess, the first glimmers of realisation entering his eyes.

'I haven't told them yet,' said Jess.

Mr Appleton looked aghast, and Jess jolly well hoped he felt aghast, too, the interfering nincompoop.

'I'm sorry,' said Mum. 'I've been engulfed by a library crisis. Do come in and have a cup of tea.'

Mr Appleton was soon comfortably installed at the kitchen table with a steaming mug of tea before him. During the transition from front door to kitchen table, Mum politely enquired how Mr Appleton's magnificent son Luke was faring, and they were told he was away – not organising African orphanages or winning Nobel Prizes for Curly Hair this time, but just visiting his girlfriend in Manchester.

'So,' said Mum, once the usual admiring remarks about Luke had been expressed, 'what was all this about Saturday night?' She looked severely at Mr Appleton.

Mr Appleton turned to Jess. 'I'm sure Jess would welcome the chance to explain,' he said gravely.

Yeah, *right*, thought Jess. *I'd welcome this like I'd welcome a scorpion in my slipper*. She did have to explain, however, and now was the moment. Reeling with dread, she forced herself to begin.

'Some people came round here on Saturday night,' she faltered, looking pleadingly at Mum, her eyes huge and yearning for forgiveness like a poodle puppy who has poodled on the carpet and is hoping to get away with it. 'I don't know why, but a rumour had gone round that there was going to be a party here and they all just turned up.'

'Gatecrashers,' said Mr Appleton firmly. 'This happens a lot nowadays, I believe. Word gets round on Facebook or Twitter or whatever, and hordes of people, complete strangers, just turn up.'

'Hordes!' said Mum faintly, turning pale.

'Not hordes!' exclaimed Jess. 'Just about . . . Well, I'm not sure. I didn't count them.'

'Probably about twenty or thirty,' said Mr Appleton. 'About a classful, I'd say.'

Jess was grateful to him for underestimating the numbers of gatecrashers. He'd massively underestimated it.

'Thirty?' gasped Mum, appalled. If only she knew. 'Who were they?'

'I didn't know any of them,' said Jess.

She was fleetingly tempted to say they might be friends of friends of friends of Mackenzie, but she didn't dare. Then her mum would set off for Mackenzie's house with as many instruments of torture as she could lay her hands on, and poor Mackenzie's chances of happiness in this life would be at an end. And, as Jess's friend, Mackenzie would confirm that Jess was in some obscure way to blame. Whereas if the gatecrashers remained obligingly anonymous, Jess would be in the clear. Well, almost.

'Somebody turned the lights down,' Jess added lamely. 'So it was kind of hard to see what they looked like anyway.'

'Those gatecrashers,' announced Granny darkly, 'have stolen my funeral fund!'

Jess had to sit through the awful details of the missing envelope again. Mum looked horrified. Perhaps she'd even temporarily forgotten about the looming library closure.

'I can't believe it!' she exclaimed. 'All this on top of the library closure!' (Oh no, she hadn't.) 'Not to mention Great-Aunt Jane's stroke.'

'Oh dear.' Mr Appleton had heard about the ailing aunt and now expressed concern. 'How did you find her?'

'Bad,' said Mum.

'It's hard to imagine she'll ever be back to her old self,' confirmed Granny grimly.

Mr Appleton looked tragic. There was a moment's pause. 'Well,' he said in his gentle coaxing way, 'perhaps that puts everything else in perspective.'

'No, it doesn't!' countered Granny fiercely. 'I could still pop off ages before Jane, if she goes lingering on.'

'Don't be silly, Granny,' said Mum. 'You're not going to pop off for ages.'

'But someone's nicked my three hundred quid!' yelled Granny.

'That is a problem.' Mr Appleton was trying to think of something pacifying to say, but it eluded him this time.

'I'll make sure you get it back, Granny,' Jess vowed, grabbing her hand. 'I was here so I feel responsible. It was my fault.'

Here she paused for one of the grown-ups to contradict her and reassure her that she was utterly blameless and divine. Curiously, they didn't. They all just looked at her – very stonily in Mum's case.

'I promise I will get your three hundred pounds back!' Jess assured her fervently.

Granny squeezed her hand and shook her head. 'Well, dear, that's all very well,' she sighed, 'but if they were all strangers, I don't see how you can possibly manage it.'

'I can manage it, Granny!' Jess insisted. 'I'll get your money back – you'll see!'

Just then Jess's mobile phone pinged. A text had arrived. She fumbled around in her pocket. It was from Mackenzie. WHAT'S THIS I HEAR ABOUT YOU 'N' FRED?

Oh no! While Jess was defending Mackenzie's honour and concealing his guilt, he was spreading rumours about her and Fred!

' 'Scuse me a minute,' Jess murmured and raced upstairs, her heart pounding.

What on earth had Mackenzie heard? Who had told anybody anything? How long would it be before whatever it was made its way to Jodie's ears? If Fred made any reference at all to his fireside chat with Jess it would be unforgivable. It would be the end of everything between them – yet again, before they'd even had the chance to resurrect their doomed double act.

Fred! What *had* he done?

Chapter 27

Jess called him immediately.

'Mackenzie, you idiot, what do you mean?' she snapped. She had to keep her voice down because of the grown-ups downstairs, otherwise she would literally have bawled.

'Hi, Jordan!' Mackenzie sounded cheeky and unrepentant. 'So how was last night? Was it all violins and roses?'

'Shut up, you doofus! Tell me what you meant by that text!' Jess was fuming.

'Oh, just that Ben came round to my place last night after he'd walked Flora home, and he said you and Fred were Left Alone Together.'

'So what? Fred was shampooing the carpet! Because of the mess made by *your* friends! I noticed that you conveniently disappeared when my house was being trashed by hordes of strangers invited by you! And where were you when we were doing the cleaning up? Which, incidentally, took hours!'

'Friends of mine?' Mackenzie laughed again, but his laugh sounded a little hollow and guilty. 'I didn't tell anybody about your party!'

'First of all, it wasn't supposed to be a party! It was supposed to be a couple of my closest friends coming round for a pizza and a DVD! Secondly, you told me yourself you'd told Owen somebody-or-other-with-a-posh-name, plus at least three other people I'd never heard of, and they obviously passed the message on, and I'm in big trouble with my mum about it, so thanks for ruining my life!'

Jess was aware that she was exaggerating slightly, as currently her mum was deep in her library crisis and hadn't even inspected her house for damage yet. But she wanted to give Mackenzie a verbal bashing because it could so easily have gone even more horribly wrong, and she also wanted to punish him for whatever he'd said about her and Fred.

'And to return to your stupid rumour about Fred and me, I hope you haven't been doing any more of your gossiping because Fred just shampooed the carpet and went home like a normal mate. End of story. I assume you've already spread your vile fantasies all over the nearest Facebook wall?'

'Don't get your knickers in a twist!' laughed Mackenzie. 'I'm only joking!'

'But did you say anything to anybody? Because Jodie's in a bad place at the moment – I hope you realise that. Her dad's having chemo, plus she's had to abandon the half-marathon, so she's got enough to cope with without malicious rumours flying about.'

'Oh, I had no idea about her dad.' Mackenzie sounded shocked. 'OK, OK, there is no story. So what are you doing later today?'

'None of your business!' said Jess. She was still furious with Mackenzie. She didn't trust him, and if she so much as bumped into him by accident later she was going to give him more grief. She rang off in a strop and considered her options. She had to go and see Jodie, and the sooner the better.

Downstairs she could hear Mr Appleton leaving. He seemed to be promising to help Mum with the Save The Library Campaign. He was a teacher so he probably loved all that stuff. Jess lurked in the bathroom for a few minutes after he'd gone, and then went down. She found Mum in the back garden. She was staring dubiously at the line of rubbish sacks.

'Well, Jess,' she said sadly, 'I'm sorry to say this is the last time you're going to be left Home Alone.'

Jess bit her tongue. She was so, so tempted to burst out in a fiery speech about how utterly innocent she was, and how hard she'd worked to clean the house up, but she realised it would only be counter-productive. So, heroically and unusually, she said nothing.

'Look at all those bin bags!' Mum shook her head in doleful distress, then turned to her beloved daffodils. 'Still, thank goodness they didn't touch my daffs.' She smiled contentedly at the jolly yellow flowers and inhaled deeply. 'I can smell their scent on the air.' Mum went all mystical for a moment. 'It's a peppery sort of smell . . . the essence of spring.'

Jess stared at the daffodils. If only Mum knew! How on earth had the daffodil patch been resurrected? Was there really a guardian angel at work? If so, they deserved five-star feedback on heaven's website.

'I'm going to see Jodie,' she said. 'She's pulled a hamstring and her dad's got cancer.'

Mum frowned and looked concerned. Jess felt as if she'd used Jodie's dad's cancer to score points against

Mum, and it made her uneasy. She wasn't sure her guardian angel would appreciate that one.

'Oh dear,' said Mum. 'Is it bad?'

'He's having chemo,' said Jess.

Mum sighed. 'How awful for them,' she murmured and went indoors.

At last she'd stopped thinking how bad Jess was at keeping hordes of strangers out of the house and started to get a sense of perspective.

The minute Jess walked into Jodie's sitting room, she knew there was trouble ahead. Jodie was lying on the sofa with her leg stretched out on a cushion. She looked up at Jess, and her expression wasn't friendly.

'Welcome to intensive care,' she practically snarled. 'Nice of you to come.' She sounded sarcastic and rather sneery.

'You poor thing!' Jess hesitated, then knelt down and gave her a hug. Jodie accepted the hug, but sort of half-resisted it, too. She certainly didn't seem pleased to see Jess.

Had she heard any rumours? Jess was walking on eggshells. If only she'd brought some chocolate.

'What's your favourite sort of chocolate?' she asked quickly. 'I'll go out and get you some.'

'Forget chocolate!' said Jodie sharply – a most unusual remark from her, as she was famously addicted to the stuff. 'If I eat chocolate while I'm stuck on this sofa, I'll get as fat as a pig again. Or maybe that's what you want?' Her look was bold and challenging. Something had certainly put her in a bad mood.

'What's the matter, Jodie?' Jess sat down on the nearest chair, trying to look saintly and concerned.

'I'm in pain, didn't you know?' Jodie glared at her leg. 'So how did the rave of the century go last night? What time did it end?'

Did Jodie know anything? Was she fishing? Had the divine Ben Jones been doing more godlike gossiping?

'It ended quite early,' said Jess. 'Basically I wanted everyone out of there because it wasn't my party. It was something Mackenzie and his stupid friends imposed on me. He's always shooting his mouth off and getting people into trouble.' She hoped Jodie would get the hidden message there. 'He just invents things. He invented the idea that I was throwing a party, and a huge crowd of strangers nearly trashed my house. If we hadn't had the idea of switching the electricity off and spreading the news about the police coming and there being another party across town, I think they'd still be there now.'

'And what's this I hear about you and Fred?' demanded Jodie.

Oh no! What had she heard? Jess could feel a blush rushing up her neck, and there was nothing she could do to stop it.

Chapter 28

'What? What about Fred?' Jess tried to make it sound perfectly innocent.

'Just something somebody said.'

'Who? Said what?' Jess was doing her best to make her voice sound completely neutral, as if she hadn't the faintest idea what Jodie was driving at. But she knew her face was bright red because she could feel her cheeks burning.

'Tiffany said she saw him arriving at your house this morning with loads and loads of flowers.'

'Oh, that!' Jess felt a huge wave of relief wash over her and a delicious delight that it had been Fred who was her guardian angel. This wasn't about their fireside chat – this was about the daffodils. 'The gate-crashers trashed my mum's daffodil patch last night, and when I got up this morning I was, like, dreading seeing it in the daylight, because my mum is basically demented about her flowers. You can trash her house, take the roof off, help yourself, no problem – but her precious daffs? Touch them and you're dead meat!' Jess felt that she was prattling away at high speed like a lorry running downhill with the brakes off, but she just had to hurtle on.

'Anyway, I woke up and went out to the garden, all poised and ready to cringe and scream, and it was amazing! I found somebody had replaced them. They'd been replanted so well, as if they'd been in our garden the whole time. I hadn't the faintest clue who'd done it, but now you say Tiffany saw Fred loaded down with flowers, I realise that I was whingeing on at him about how my mum was addicted to her flower bed, and he must've decided to wave his magic wand and replace them!'

'It's unusual for Fred to be so thoughtful.' Jodie sounded faintly bitter.

'I expect it was kind of like a practical joke to him. He must have come in through the back gate – you know you can get into my garden down a side passage and round the back, right?'

'So they weren't flowers for you?'

'Of course not! They were flowers for my mum.' Jess felt her blush beginning to fade. 'Fred has a big thing going with my mum, of course. He worships the ground she walks on. No, wait! It's vice versa. Mum worships Fred. I find it rather tiresome. Frankly I don't know what he sees in her. Maybe it's the wooden earrings shaped like parrots and the mad, middle-aged moustache.' Jess was obviously exaggerating her mum's beauty and style for comic effect. She wanted to get Jodie to smile. But Jodie still looked bad-tempered and suspicious.

'So why are you blushing?'

'I just blush all the time. About nothing. I can't help it. I blush when I see snogging in films. I blush when a puppy dog widdles on my shoe. I blush when I fail the maths test. I blush when I pass the maths test. I blush when somebody says the word *lavatory*. That's all.'

'Oh yeah?' Jodie was surly and unconvinced.

'Listen, Jodie.' Jess decided a descent into the more-or-less truth was required. 'It's embarrassing when you say the word *Fred*. There's a history there. I can't deny it. But I dumped Fred, remember? I dumped him fair and square. He was free to do anything he liked and to go out with anybody he liked. And . . .' Jess hesitated. It felt so odd to be speaking the truth, but it also felt like the most tremendous relief. 'To be honest,' she went on swiftly, 'I completely understand why he picked you. Why wouldn't he? You're funny and you're pretty and you've got a load of attitude. So it's totally and utterly fine. But it is still a little bit, well, awkward when you suddenly glare at me and say, "What's this I hear about you and Fred?" It's kind of a delicate subject, don't you see that?'

Jodie reflected for a moment, then reached out and grabbed Jess's hand. 'Thanks, Jess,' she said, smiling at last. 'Sorry I'm such a grouch at the moment. Lying here on my own, I just keep thinking weird thoughts.'

Jess squeezed her hand and beamed.

Suddenly the doorbell rang.

'Would you mind getting that, Jess?' asked Jodie, shifting uncomfortably on her sofa. 'I think my mum's in the shower.'

Jess jumped up and went to the door. Somehow she was expecting it to be a friend of Jodie's family, a stranger, or some random person from Planet Elsewhere.

But disaster! It was Fred standing there, carrying a bunch of flowers. He flinched slightly at the sight of her – he'd obviously been expecting somebody else, too. Jess hadn't seen him since late, late last night, when she'd been lying on the sofa staring into his eyes and sleep had finally overcome her. At the sight of the bunch of flowers, her hand twitched slightly towards him, even though she knew in an instant the flowers were meant for Jodie. She changed the hand twitch to a hair-smoothing exercise and tried to look cool and composed. It was impossible.

'Oh!' she faltered. 'Ah! The Flower Man!'

'I never want to see another flower as long as I live,' muttered Fred, stumbling in over the doormat and then, in the hall, hesitating and turning back to her.

They both realised that every word they said would be heard by poor Jodie, lurking on her sofa of pain in the next room.

'Hey! They tell me it was you who replaced my mum's daffs!' said Jess, trying to sound bright and friendly but somehow distant and neutral, as if she'd met Fred a few times, not been all that impressed and could hardly remember his name. 'Thanks so much! That was brilliant! She never suspected a thing!'

Fred shrugged and looked distracted and furtive. 'Good,' he said. Then he went into the sitting room, turned to Jodie and tossed the bunch of flowers lightly into her lap. 'Put that in your pipe and smoke it!' he said with an uncomfortable grin.

'Oooooh!' Jodie beamed, grabbing them and inhaling deeply. 'Don't they smell fab!'

'Shall I put them in water for you, Jodie?' asked Jess, anxious to escape from the room for a moment.

Jodie and Fred looked deeply embarrassed. A kiss would have been on the cards, but with Jess standing there watching like some terrible old stuffed bird of prey, that was obviously an impossibility. Jess grabbed the flowers and ran out to the kitchen.

The flowers were narcissi, like tiny daffs, and they were pumping out the most gorgeous scent in the world. It was the smell of sunshine and spring and blue skies and soft breezes. It flooded through Jess's lungs and seemed to caress her, trying to persuade her to cheer up and remember that life was full of rainbows and bluebirds. But it was kind of hard to listen to the flowers' cheerful message right now, with her heart full of agitation.

She ripped the flowers' wrapping open, found a vase and turned on the tap. She wanted to make a noise of some sort because the silence from the sitting room was deafening. Were Fred and Jodie locked in a passionate embrace? How long should she wait before going back there? Should she sing loudly on her way back to warn them? If so, what song would be suitable? Lost in her panicky brain fog, Jess could only think of *God Save the Queen*. It would be hard to trill that jauntily and still look uber cool.

She found a pair of scissors and cut off the ends of the narcissus stalks, because Granny had once told her it made the flowers last longer. She wanted to spend at least twenty minutes arranging them or, even better, thirty years; that would be ideal, because she didn't want to have to go back into Jodie's sitting room ever again.

So she started arranging the flowers, one by one, with infinite care, silently asking each bloom how it was today. There was the murmur of voices from the sitting room now, which was encouraging, though Jess couldn't hear what they were saying. She was racked with the desire to eavesdrop shamelessly. She would so love to see what was happening while remaining invisible herself, as a fly on the wall, or by crouching behind the sofa.

Maybe they were deliberately whispering. Maybe they were talking about her! Jess was feeling so terribly spare, like a hanger-on or a gooseberry. It was a bit much for her to feel like she was chaperoning her ex with his latest girlfriend.

Eventually Jess filled the vase with flowers – however much of a perfectionist you are, it's hard to take a week over that particular task – and, having got rid of the wrapper and the cut stalks and wiped down the work surface incredibly slowly, she felt she had no choice but to rejoin Fred and Jodie.

Fred was sitting on the floor beside the sofa, half-leaning on it, but there was no hand-holding or canoodling of any kind going on, thank goodness. Jess couldn't wait to make an excuse and leave.

'Where shall I put them?' she asked, brandishing the flowers.

'On the coffee table, right next to me!' commanded Jodie, moving her magazines. 'Mmm, that smell! Wow!'

Jess carefully placed the vase on the coffee table and then hesitated. 'I should be going,' she faltered, looking towards the door.

'What?' cried Jodie. 'No, Jess! You've only just arrived! I wanna hear all about the party! Sit down and give me the goss!'

Jess selected a low stool and crashed down on it with all the grace of a tired elephant. It seemed she would have to endure yet more absolute torment.

Chapter 29

Jess told the whole story of the party, and Jodie listened avidly.

'What a nightmare!' she gasped. 'How terrible! If it had happened here, I wouldn't have had a clue what to do!'

'It was Ben Jones's idea which saved the day!' explained Jess.

'Er, no, I think it was mine,' countered Fred.

'Wasn't it Ben who suggested we turn the electricity off?' said Jess. 'I know you always want the credit for everything, Parsons, but it was Ben who suggested the faux power cut.'

'No, no, it was me! And also I ran through the house screeching about some other party where attractive mayhem was available.'

'OK, I admit that.'

'And I helped to clean up afterwards.'

'Well, you shampooed a carpet or two, but you'd probably have been doing that on a Saturday night anyway.'

'I'm famous for my housework!' boasted Fred.

'So what time did it all end?' asked Jodie.

Jess's heart gave an anxious little skip. Talking about the party was easy. Talking about the clearing up was OK because Ben Jones and Flora had been there. But talking about when the evening had ended was a dodgy subject.

'It was all over by about midnight,' said Jess. 'Thank goodness, because I think if it had gone on any later one of the neighbours might have called the police.' She put on a posh 1930s voice. 'One doesn't want the police turning up at one's parties – they lower the tone.' Jess wondered if she could steer the conversation away from the events of the previous evening and towards the police as party animals. 'Police uniforms, right?' she ploughed on. 'I think they're quite cool. Not when they're wearing the bulletproof waistcoats, though – that creates an undesirable chunky look.'

'I prefer postmen's uniforms,' said Fred. 'More casual. And they can wear shorts all summer. Though personally I can't wear shorts as my knees are so knobbly. I've had an ASBO slapped on me for wearing shorts in public.'

'What's an ASBO?' asked Jodie.

'An Antisocial Behaviour Order,' Fred informed her. 'Wearing shorts is definitely antisocial if you have legs like mine.'

'My dad's a postman,' said Jess, aware that this conversation about uniforms had a surreal quality. She wanted to be talking about something ordinary, but was unsure how to get there. 'I don't think Dad's ever going to wear shorts, though, unless it's compulsory.'

'I never used to wear shorts,' said Jodie, 'because my knees are as fat as anything, but I was going to wear some for the half-marathon.'

'But you've lost loads of weight since you've been running,' Jess told her. 'You'd look great in shorts. You don't need the excuse of the half-marathon. Wear some anyway!'

'I'm furious about the half-marathon,' sighed Jodie, leaning back and glaring at the ceiling.

Jess felt the conversation was going a bit better now, towards subjects which were real but not dangerous.

'Fred will have to do it on his own. Unless you'd take my place?' Jodie sat up suddenly and stared at Jess.

'I couldn't possibly do the half-marathon!' Jess

protested. 'I mean, I'm totally unfit – I get puffed just running upstairs.'

'But I was going to collect so much money for Cancer Research!' lamented Jodie.

'I know,' said Jess, 'but maybe you could get all those people who were going to sponsor you to sponsor you for doing something else.'

'They could sponsor you for lying on the sofa,' suggested Fred.

For once Jodie didn't laugh.

'Jodie, I would take over your sponsors and do the half-marathon,' said Jess, feeling annoyed with herself for being so spineless, 'but I know I'd have to drop out after about ten minutes. Honestly, I'm so unfit! I'd be a total disgrace and all your sponsors would be disgusted.'

Jodie stared at the ceiling for a while, apparently deep in thought.

'I'll do anything else,' Jess offered. 'Anything. Just say the word and I'll do it. But not running.'

Jodie sat up straight again and stared at Jess with a curious expression in her eyes. 'Right! Brilliant! How about . . . walking down the high street in your undies?'

Jess screamed. 'Ugh! That would be like a horrible

nightmare! Hey, the aim is to raise money, not to get me arrested!'

'You could do a sponsored head-shave,' suggested Fred.

Jess's hands flew to her scalp. Much as she longed to help Jodie and wanted to please her sponsors, and though her hair was definitely not one of her best features (since it resembled a bramble patch), she couldn't face the thought of losing it.

'I know loads of people lose their hair for various reasons,' she said, 'and I know some girls look great bald, but seriously, if I had to lose my hair I think I'd lose my mind, too! I'd rather run down the high street without clothes than have clothes but no hair.'

'If you did think of something really amazing,' said Jodie thoughtfully, 'maybe you could get loads more sponsors as well as taking over mine. It would have to be something really unusual, though. Hey!' She grabbed her laptop. 'Let's google it!'

Jodie did a search on *crazy sponsored stunts* and got caught up in a maze of videos involving cars flipping over and turning somersaults.

'Drop the word *stunts*,' suggested Fred. 'And add the word *charity*.'

'Walk to the North Pole?!' cried Jess, looking over

Jodie's shoulder. 'In your dreams! Just walking to the fridge is my limit in terms of exercise with a dash of ice.'

'Bungee-jumping!' yelled Jodie. 'Jess, I'd seriously love to see you doing that!'

'I'd rather be coated in dog food and thrown to a pack of Rottweilers than go bungee-jumping!' screeched Jess.

'Coated in dog food. Hmmm, that sounds promising,' said Fred. 'Or you could be wrapped in a coat of dead rodents and thrown to a pack of owls.'

'I can't do bungee-jumping, I'm sorry,' said Jess. 'Just looking out of the bathroom window makes me feel giddy. I have a terrible head for heights.'

'I used to have a terrible head for heights,' mused Fred, 'and unfortunately I just kept on growing. When I first reached six feet, I had to go around with my eyes closed for a while because I was scared of falling off my own face.'

It soon be came clear that the internet didn't offer much in the way of really inspiring ideas. Somebody was indeed shaving her head. Somebody else was growing a beard.

'You could grow a beard,' suggested Fred. 'Oh, sorry – you already have.'

'To be honest,' sighed Jess, 'none of these ideas is any good. Tell you what, Jodie – I'll go away and have a think.'

Jess got to her feet. She had to come up with a great idea for raising money and felt she needed to be on her own to get inspired. She was determined to think of something amazing to help Jodie and her dad – preferably something that didn't hurt or require her to cut off part of her body.

'I'm a bit tired after clearing up after last night,' she explained. 'And I promised I'd get back to help my mum plan her campaign.' This was a lie, but only a white one, as Jess was sure Jodie and Fred wanted to be left alone together. 'They're going to close the library, so my mum will be out of a job.'

'Close the library?' Fred looked shocked. 'Where are we going to go after school to mess about and look for books about weird and rude things?'

Jess shrugged.

'What will your mum do?' asked Jodie. 'Maybe she could get a job in a bookshop?'

'Maybe,' said Jess. 'But first she's going to fight one of her legendary campaigns to try and keep the library open.'

'Well, count me in!' said Jodie. 'Once my stupid

leg's better, tell your mum I'll do anything I can to help.'

Jess thanked Jodie and headed for the door. As she said goodbye, she found herself taking a mental snap-shot of Jodie and Fred together: Jodie sprawling on the sofa, Fred sitting on the floor. In her head a voice was saying, in a *Wuthering Heights*-y sort of way, '*Mr Frederick Parsons and Miss Jodie Gordon having announced their engagement, Miss Jessica Jordan paused by the door, her dark eyes flashing, to bid them farewell. Mr Parsons felt her gaze pierce his very soul . . .*'

'See ya, then!' said Jess cheerily and stepped out into what had mysteriously become a thick fog.

Chapter 30

The weather had changed dramatically: the wind had dropped, the temperature had risen slightly and the fog had come rolling up. Jess could hardly see the houses on the opposite side of the road. However, she knew the way home – she reckoned she could have walked it blindfolded – so she set off, glad to be alone and almost enjoying being enveloped by whiteness.

People walking past seemed to suddenly loom up at her and then vanish, which was spooky, especially as it was the middle of the day, but it was kind of exciting. There was a choice of route home: Jess could either walk the quickest way, down various streets, or go a slightly longer route through the park. She chose the park.

For a start, she needed to think. She had so much on her agenda that her mind was reeling. First, there was the stuff at home: Mum's likely unemployment, Granny's missing £300, the disappearance of Rasputin and the repercussions of the party. Then there was the whole Jodie business. At the same time as acquiring Jess's former boyfriend, Jodie seemed to have got rid of her most onerous chore – some kind of sponsored ordeal in aid of charity. Jess hated herself for thinking of it like this, because Jodie really did deserve sympathy. Her dad was very ill, and she herself was immobilised and in pain. OK, she was stuck on a sofa with Fred – not too bad as destinies go – but she couldn't stroll through the park as Jess was doing now.

Jess took a few deep breaths and slowed down. Trees were dotted about, cloaked in fog, their shapes sinister and vague. Figures passed by, indistinct, like people drawn in pencil, colourless and lost. The atmosphere was dreamy, and through it all Jess could hear the peacocks calling with their echoing cry. The park had ornamental fowl in enclosures by the lake: there were flotillas of jolly little ducks, strange golden pheasants, and the peacocks, who roosted in a cedar tree.

It felt rather liberating to be here, away from home, away from Jodie and Fred, away from everybody who was doing her head in. Jess switched off her mobile phone and gave herself up to her own thoughts. Despite being almost lost, and despite her crowded agenda, she felt strangely happy. If she could feel this sense of ease on her own, maybe that was a sign. Perhaps if she stopped wanting to be back with Fred, she'd recover her energy and feel comfortable in her own life again.

Jodie needed Fred far more than she did right now. Jess's parents weren't ill, thank goodness. Even her Granny was reassuringly sprightly. And Jess's own legs worked.

Through the fog, Jess heard a distant cry. It seemed that someone was calling her name. She paused for a moment to listen more intently. Nobody knew she was here. Nobody could possibly recognise her in this fog. In fact, nobody could even see her. Jess listened. It came again, but this time in a slightly different direction and further off: 'Jess! Jess!'

She didn't know whether to answer or not. It seemed ridiculous to call a reply, especially when lots of girls are called Jess. So she kept quiet and just went on strolling through the foggy park, roughly in the direction of the bandstand.

A little dog appeared before her. It was some kind of terrier; a mixed breed, brown and furry. It wagged its tail and looked up at her.

'Hello, darling!' cried Jess in delight.

The dog's tail wagged some more. Jess bent down to stroke it. The inquisitive black nose snuffled and snortled around Jess's boots. She looked about for the dog's owner, but there was nobody to be seen.

The dog was wearing a collar and there was an identity medal hanging from it. It said, *My name is Jess and I'm microchipped.* On the other side were the name and contact details of the owner, Mrs Beatrice Finch, with a phone number.

Jess was leaping up on her hind legs, begging for attention. (Dog Jess, not Human Jess.) Jess picked her up, and the two Jesses enjoyed a little cuddle in the middle of the foggy park. The dog smelled nice. There were tiny beads of fog vapour on her fur, but beneath she was warm and wriggly.

'Where's your owner, Jess?' she asked, nuzzling Jess's neck where the fur was very thick. The other Jess didn't offer any reply. 'I think I'd better phone her,' said Jess. 'You get down now and don't run off. Stay by me.'

She put Jess down and got out her mobile. The dog stood obediently close to her legs. She seemed to have taken a fancy to Jess the Human.

'Oh well,' sighed Jess, dialling Mrs Finch's number. 'At least I appear to be attractive to canines.'

'Hello?' Mrs Finch's voice was deep and husky.

'I think I've found your dog in the park,' said Jess.

'Oh, thank you! Thank you!' gushed Mrs Finch. 'I was calling and calling for her – the silly little thing ran off. Where are you now?'

'Well, I'm not sure where I am exactly,' confessed Jess. 'The fog's so thick! But I think I'm fairly near the bandstand by the far end of the lake. I can hear the ducks quacking.'

'I'll meet you by the bandstand, then, shall I?' asked Mrs Finch. 'Sorry, what's your name?'

'My name's Jess, too,' said Jess, laughing.

'How strange and delightful!' said Mrs Finch. She sounded like a posh teacher or something. 'I'll see you there in a few minutes, then. It might be best to carry her in case she runs off again – if you don't mind?'

Jess didn't mind at all – it was like having a living teddy bear to hug – and she walked on towards the bandstand with her face buried in Jess's fur. Soon the vague shape of the bandstand emerged from the fog, and Jess remembered all the times she had met Fred here – and also met Luke, the boy next door, when she'd been trying in vain to fall for him. She recalled Luke's smart aviator jacket, his adorable curls, his pouty lips, and how, though she liked him a great deal, there had always been something missing. Whereas Fred, with his gangling frame, his long, stick-like legs and his hunched shoulders . . . Jess's heart gave a tiny kick at the memory of Fred mooching towards her. But no! She mustn't think like that! Fred was Jodie's boyfriend now, and she needed him, and Jess was going to be fine about it.

She reached the bandstand first and waited, cuddling the little dog. Eventually a middle-aged woman appeared through the fog. Her dark hair was rumpled, her glasses were held together with sticky tape, and she was wearing a hobo coat that had clearly been acquired at a charity shop. But she had a kind smile, and when Jess the dog saw her, she wriggled out of Jess the girl's arms, jumped down and ran to her.

Mrs Finch bent down and secured Jess to her lead, then she smiled gratefully. 'Thank you so, so much for rescuing her!' she said. 'I was totally distraught. She never normally runs off like that. And how strange that you should be called Jess! Are you quite real? Or are you Jess's guardian angel?'

'No, I'm not a guardian angel.' Jess smiled. 'In fact, I could do with one myself at the moment.'

Mrs Finch giggled merrily. 'Well, I wish I could do

you a favour in return. If you ever need a fairy godmother, here's my card.' She fished a card out of her bag. It was ever so slightly grubby. 'Sorry, it's dog-eared. A bit like Jess. If you ever need a speech give me a call – I write speeches, you see, for weddings and so on. You never know . . .' Mrs Finch smiled. 'I'm so grateful!'

'It was fun,' said Jess. 'Lovely to meet you – and Jess!'

She gave the little dog a last caress and then they parted because, despite a strong feeling of friendliness on both sides, it was hard to see where the relationship could go from there.

Just then, out of the blue – or rather, out of the white – an idea flashed into Jess's mind. She grabbed her phone and called Flora.

'Hey, Flo!' she cried. 'What say we do the half-marathon, but we walk it, and I'll be dressed as a dog on a lead?'

Chapter 31

The idea of taking Jess dressed as a dog for a thirteen mile walk for charity appealed to Flora immediately. Jess walked home feeling slightly more hopeful. She'd found a way to help Jodie which wasn't going to be too awful. Compared to the horrors of bungee-jumping, walking about dressed as a dog would be easy-peasy. Jess felt that, if required, she was quite prepared to walk right around the world wearing a diamanté collar and lead.

As she let herself in through the front door, she heard raised voices in the kitchen. She closed the door softly behind her and immediately started to eavesdrop. It was Dad and Mum. He must have come round to welcome her home, hoping to be thanked for ironing her paperwork, and instead found that he'd walked into a war zone, poor guy.

'I know I've contributed very little in the past,' he was saying, 'but it's going to be different from now on. You can depend on me.'

'But, Tim, Jess will be living at home for several more years and then there's college – if she thinks she can face the student loan.' Mum's voice was rising with barely suppressed hysteria. Jess started feeling guilty for even existing. 'It's not a question of your helping a bit more,' Mum went on. 'It's a question of whether or not I can hold on to the house.'

'Surely it's not that bad?'

'But if I lose my job how can I pay the mortgage?'

'You'll find a new job, Madeleine. And you can probably get benefits while you're looking.'

'You can't get housing benefits for a mortgage, Tim!' Mum was evidently much more clued up than Dad. 'I'll have to sell the house! We'll have to move somewhere cheaper – maybe rent somewhere.'

'Well, it's not the end of the world,' said Dad firmly. 'I've just done it. I had to give up a fabulous house in St Ives, get a job and rent a tiny flat overlooking a car park. And it's fine.'

'But, Tim, you're on your own! I've got two dependants.'

'You're not struggling on your own,' said Dad. 'I

really will help. Postmen earn about the same as librarians. I can contribute. And you may not lose your job. If we can put up a real fight and get the community behind us, they may decide to keep the library open.'

There was a brief silence, during which Mum sighed. Jess stealthily took off her jacket and hung it on the peg.

'Jess!' called Mum. 'Is that you?'

'No!' called Jess, trying to lighten the mood. 'It's the mad axe murderer! But you're in luck: I don't work on Sundays. Even axe murderers have days off.'

She entered the kitchen. Her parents looked slightly furtive.

'We're discussing the situation,' said Mum, with a hunted air.

'I know, I've been eavesdropping out there for ages,' said Jess, trying to be cheerful. 'And may I say what a disappointment you are! Most couples would be hurling plates by now, but you just sound vaguely tetchy. Seriously, Mum, don't worry about money. If you lose your job I'll leave school in the summer and get a job as a dog walker.'

'You will not leave school in the summer!' snarled her mum, half-rising from her chair in fury and outrage. 'You're going to have a decent education even if we have to pay for it for the rest of our lives!'

'From what I've heard,' said Jess lightly, 'we'll still be paying for it in two hundred years. Whatever! It's still worth it for the chance to go to uni and blow my whole loan on shoes!'

'Jess!' cried her mum, looking dismayed.

'She's only joking, Madeleine,' said Dad gently. 'Trying to cheer us up a bit.'

He reached across the table and squeezed Mum's hand. Mum looked startled, then, after a moment's thought, she seemed to soften a little. She didn't take her hand away, either. Jess felt a strange small dance of delight in her heart. Seeing her parents holding hands, after everything they'd been through, was touching.

Jess had always thought of Mum as the responsible one, and of Dad as the one who went off and did what he wanted in a bohemian kind of way. But he seemed to have changed – grown up a bit. Being dumped by Phil had clearly done him good. But had being dumped by Jess done Fred any good? The jury was still out on that one.

'Tea, anyone?' asked Jess, strolling to the kettle.

'Oh, yes, please, Jess,' said Mum. 'At least we can still afford a cuppa.'

'This is happening to everyone, Mum,' said Jess. 'Flora's dad's business went bust, remember, and they had to sell their posh house and now they live in an ordinary house just like ours, and her mum's got a job, and I think, if anything, they're happier.'

'Yes, yes.' Mum nodded. 'So . . .' She clearly wanted to change the subject. She turned to Dad and they stopped holding hands, as if they'd reached a natural breaking-off point. 'Let's talk about something else . . . You're redecorating your bathroom, Tim. What colour are you painting it?'

'Blue,' said Dad with a broad grin. 'A kind of soft pale blue, like the ocean seen through mist.'

'Don't get him on the subject of blue, Mum!' Jess warned. 'Don't forget, Dad lived by the sea for years.'

'I wish I could do something about my study,' said Mum. 'The wallpaper's falling off – it's a disgrace.'

'You could let me paint it for you!' said Dad excitedly. He'd been waiting for this opportunity. 'And to celebrate the next anniversary of our doomed marriage, I'll pay for the paint.'

Mum gave a rueful unconvinced smile. 'I've got such a lot on my plate now,' she sighed. 'It doesn't seem the moment to redecorate.'

'I think it's the perfect moment, Mum!' Jess was

keen to back her dad up. 'We can all help. It'll make everything feel fresh and new. I love painting! In fact, this afternoon I want to go and give Dad a hand to paint his bathroom – if you haven't finished it yet, Daddo?'

'No,' said Dad. 'I've left it for you.'

'You can only go to Dad's if you've done your homework,' warned Mum, resuming her usual dreary regime of nagging.

'Of course I've done my homework,' lied Jess. 'I did it on Friday night, don't you remember?'

Mum frowned. She clearly couldn't remember what had happened on Friday night. Dad gave Jess a querying sort of look, because she'd been at his house and he obviously couldn't remember her doing any homework, but he was sporting enough not to interrogate her further at this point.

Shortly afterwards, as she walked over to Dad's place with him, he did commence a little questioning.

'So what's the homework situation really?' he asked.

'Oh, it's nothing!' breezed Jess. 'Don't worry! I can do it when I get back! I could do it with my eyes closed! I could do it in a split second! It's only English, and you know I love writing essays!'

Dad looked dubious and sighed to himself. Then he gave a defeated kind of shrug and turned to other matters. 'How were things with what's-her-name? Jackie?'

'Jodie, Dad!' Jess laughed. He was hopeless at names. 'She was fine. In fact, we had a bit of a girly heart-to-heart before Fred arrived.'

'And after Fred arrived? Was it OK?'

'Yes. Plus I've offered to take Jodie's place in the half-marathon so she won't lose her sponsors for Cancer Research. I'm going to walk it – literally – and I'll be dressed as a dog.'

Dad stopped and stared at her. 'Where are you going to get a dog costume?' he asked.

'Well, you know you said you were still in touch with Phil? Like, it's sort of amicable between you guys?'

'Yes, it's fine.'

'Well, I was rather hoping he'd be able to lend me one.' Phil had worked in the theatre in the past and was totally into clothes and costumes of all sorts.

'Oh, I'm sure that'll be OK,' said Dad. 'I'll ring him when we get home.'

'So it's already home to you, Dad, is it?' asked Jess. 'That's good.'

'I can make myself at home anywhere,' said Dad. 'I

think Mum will have trouble, though, if she has to leave your present house. She's been there for years and really put roots down. And I don't suppose you can remember living anywhere else. We'll just have to make sure you can stay there. We'll have to think of something.'

He sounded determined. Jess was beginning to think that Dad was a tower of strength in a crisis after all, and not, as she had previously assumed, a strand of overcooked spaghetti.

'Right, Dad!' she beamed, taking his arm as they walked along and squeezing it. 'Thinking caps on!'

Back at Dad's flat, Jess dived into her painting gear – an old shirt of Grandpa's, already liberally spattered with paint. Then they attacked the bathroom: Dad did the complicated woodwork bits such as the window frames, while Jess had the best time rolling lovely light fresh blue all over the previous shrieking orange. As the orange colour disappeared, Jess could feel herself becoming calmer.

Until, that was, the doorbell rang.

'Strange,' said Dad, pausing. 'I'm not expecting anybody.' He was kneeling on the window sill at the time, painting the top of the window frame. 'Would you mind getting that?'

Jess put down her roller and walked to the door. She was bundled up in raggedy paint-spattered clothing, and as she neared the front door she smoothed her hair back in a small concession to style. She looked like something not even a charity shop would accept, but, hey, who cared! Whoever had rung the bell couldn't be that important.

But it was Fred.

Chapter 32

'Hi,' said Fred. 'Love the painted hair! Did you do it yourself or was it a salon job?'

'Oh!' Jess looked at her hands. They were streaked with blue. 'Is there much of it?'

'Just the odd streak,' said Fred. 'It's quite stylish.'

Then there was an awkward pause. It was extraordinary to see Fred here. How had he known where Dad lived? Something very remarkable must have happened to cause him to come. And yet his greeting had been quite skittish. If the reason for his visit had been really momentous, he wouldn't have made playful references to her painted hair.

'Come in,' said Jess. It seemed the best place to start.

Fred entered the flat in his usual incompetent way, bumping his shoulder on the door frame and tripping over the mat.

'We're painting the bathroom,' Jess explained. 'Come and see!'

Dad was getting down off the window sill. He beamed at Fred. 'Hi, Fred! I would shake hands with you but I'm covered in paint. How are you?'

'Good,' replied Fred. 'Never better, in fact.'

'I hear you're doing the half-marathon?' said Dad. Fred nodded.

'I'm doing it, too!' boasted Jess. 'I had the idea on the way home from Jodie's. I met this cute little dog in the park, and she was called Jess –'

'Spooky!' commented Fred.

'Yeah, well, I suddenly had this idea that I could walk the half-marathon dressed as a dog. And Phil's going to get me a costume. I hope it's a poodle suit.'

'I'm so jealous!' cried Fred. 'Could he get me a dog outfit, too?'

Fred seemed in very high spirits. Jess couldn't work out exactly how he was different, but there was something about him, a kind of energy which she hadn't seen for a while.

'Wouldn't you get rather hot, running in a dog costume?' asked Dad quizzically.

'No, no!' beamed Fred. 'But if I did, I could

collapse and the organisers would have to call a vet and have me put down. I might even get a spot on the news.'

'Fred, would you like a can of Coke or something?' asked Dad. 'Or an orange juice?'

'What I'd really like is a can of paint. Not to drink, obviously, though I do quite like a glass of chilled white gloss on a summer evening,' said Fred. 'Can I help?'

'Sure!' said Dad. 'But I'd better find you some old clothes of mine first.' He put down his brush and went off to his bedroom.

A huge silence developed in the bathroom. Fred was looking down at Jess. His eyes were dancing.

'What is it?' whispered Jess. 'What's happened?'

'Jodie's dumped me,' he murmured.

A flash flood of shock surged through Jess's veins. She felt amazement, joy and anxiety all at once. Jodie had dumped Fred? Why? Did she know about the fireside chat? Was she furious? Was there going to be a huge bust-up? Was Jodie even now writing all kinds of poisonous gossip on her Facebook wall?

Just then, Dad returned, carrying a big old shirt which he offered to Fred. Fred dived into it and accepted the challenge of painting the door.

'It's white, your favourite,' said Dad. 'But it's not gloss – this is the low-odour eco-friendly alternative.'

'But of course!' said Jess. 'Dad, you're the bee's knees when it comes to paint. Where you lead, the rest of the world will follow.'

'I wish I did rule the world sometimes,' sighed Dad longingly. 'There would be peace and love all round, and no bathrooms would be painted orange, ever.'

'That's just Dad's little prejudice,' Jess informed Fred. 'If your bathroom happens to be orange, don't be offended. Citrus is all the rage in some circles. Plus it's very high in vitamin C.'

They painted on for about half an hour, with Fred's recent news fizzing between them, until the bathroom was completely blue and white. Not a shred of orange remained. It looked stunning.

At this point, Fred's mobile chirped.

'I have to go,' he said. 'Got to do stuff at home. I forgot I'd promised to help my mum with the veg for tonight's big roast.'

'Enjoy it, then!' said Jess. She saw him to the door, hoping for more whispered details about the break-up, but Dad was pottering about in the background and she could see that, with an audience present, Fred wasn't in the mood for confidences.

'I'll call you tonight, possibly,' said Fred. 'Will you be back at your mum's? Your lifestyle is so glamorous. So many houses.'

'I'll be there,' Jess assured him, 'doing my homework. Mum will be in her study, so don't use the landline.' They both knew that conversations on Jess's landline could be overheard from two different directions at once: Granny downstairs and Mum on the first floor. 'Skype me maybe?' suggested Jess.

Fred nodded, stared into her eyes for a split second, and was gone.

'Nice to see Fred,' observed Dad, obviously desperate for any juicy details Jess might feel like divulging. 'He seemed to be very happy . . . ?'

'Oh, he was just his normal self.' Jess didn't really want to reveal what Fred had said in case there were going to be any repercussions. Jodie was an intense person with a violent temper. Anything could be about to happen.

Dad looked curious and he was smiling in an inviting kind of way, but Jess just shook her head and kept her mouth firmly shut.

'No news on the Fred front, then? This was just a social call?' Dad persisted.

'Exactly!' Jess confirmed.

'Oh, right. OK, then.' Dad seemed to change his train of thought. 'I've been thinking, Jess. I've had an idea which could totally sort out the situation at Mum's. But it requires you to be very, very generous indeed – almost heroically so.'

'Generous?' repeated Jess suspiciously. Though at heart a generous person, she didn't really like the sound of this. She liked being able to choose to be generous, not to have generosity forced on her. What bombshell was Dad about to drop?

'Yes,' said Dad ominously. 'I'm afraid it will hurt a little.'

Chapter 33

'I've been thinking of ways of helping Mum out,' Dad began, putting on the kettle. 'We don't want her running about like a headless chicken, do we?'

'No way!' Still Jess waited, holding her breath.

'Obviously we're hoping they won't close the library and she won't lose her job. If she does, we're hoping she'll find another job very soon.'

'Obvs!'

'But let's take the worst-case scenario. The library has to close, Mum's unemployed and she doesn't manage to get another job immediately. That's the point at which, she was saying earlier, she'd have to think about selling the house.'

'And . . . ?' Jess wanted him to get to the point.

Dad was wearing a mysterious smile. He looked very pleased with himself. 'Well, think about the accommodation there for a minute. There's Mum's bedroom, which is tiny. There are her study and the middle bedroom, which are medium-sized. And there's your front bedroom, which is huge.'

'She told me I could have that room!' cried Jess in alarm. 'It was when Granny came to live with us and I had to give up my room for her. Mum said I could have the best bedroom so she moved out into the little bedroom.'

'Kind and unselfish of her, wasn't it?'

'Well, she does have two rooms all to herself! She's got the study as well!'

'Precisely. And that seems a bit of a waste, doesn't it?'

'Dad, will you please tell me, in simple words, what you're driving at? This is making my head spin.' Jess sat down on the sofa and accepted a mug of tea.

'OK.' Dad sat down beside her. 'My plan is this. You offer Mum her front bedroom back, which is so big she'd be able to combine it with her study. She could get rid of loads of those papers in her study anyway. I realised while I was sorting out the paper-work the other night that there are box files in there stuffed with all kinds of info from her past campaigns. Stuff she can't possibly need any more, going way,

way back, like the time she helped Napoleon get elected.'

'But what? But where? How does this help?'

'If Mum has a study-bedroom in the front room and you go into the little bedroom at the back, that frees up the middle room, currently the study, and I could go in there.'

'You!' Jess was shocked – scandalised, even. 'Why?'

'I've got an income,' said Dad simply. 'Sorry to boast, but it's still a bit of a novelty to me. I've got an income, so I could pay the mortgage till Mum manages to get another job. It would only be temporary. Just to help out and not to have to sell the house.'

'But I'd have that tiny room at the back?' Jess was dismayed. 'Where would I put all my stuff?'

'Well, Mum's been in there for a while and she's not complaining,' said Dad.

'But, Dad, it's microscopic!' Jess was struggling to be generous and she couldn't help feeling desperately disappointed.

'Oh, all right, then!' Dad snapped slightly at this point – just a meek and mild, soft and furry snap, the sort a dormouse might produce if the other dormice tried to hog all the duvet. 'I'll sleep in the box room if it's too small and cramped for Lady Muck!'

'No, no, it's OK,' said Jess, ashamed. 'I'll do it, no problem. But what about this flat of yours? You'd give up this lovely flat and live in a shoebox just for us?'

'Well, I'd live in a dustbin just for you guys,' said Dad, 'but let's hope it won't come to that. Remember, we're talking several months down the line. It'll take ages for the powers that be to decide whether to close the library or not, and then Mum might get another job right away . . . A lot could happen. My tenancy at this flat is only for six months. I could be ready to move out by the end of the summer. This is just Plan B. It may never need to happen.'

'Would you be OK . . . sharing with Mum again?'

'Sure! I think we've become quite good mates. And it wouldn't be permanent.'

Jess thought how weird it would be, having her parents both living under the same roof. It would almost be like being a normal family at last.

'OK.' She leaned back and grinned. 'You've convinced me. I'll even sleep in the garden shed if it helps.' For a brief moment she imagined how idyllic it would be to live in the garden shed, though every time you turned over in bed you might be poked by the watering can.

'Don't say anything about this to Mum,' Dad

warned. 'I'll do that. It has to be introduced very diplomatically. I might even float the idea past Granny first, get her on my side.'

'My lips are sealed,' Jess promised, but almost immediately opened them to sip her tea. 'It's a great idea, Daddo. You're my knight on a white charger!'

'Heaven forbid.' Dad shuddered. 'I'm terrified of horses.'

Back home, Mum was in her study. Jess put her head round the door.

'Would you like some French toast, Mum?' she asked. It was one of Jess's specialities. Her only speciality, to be honest.

Mum looked tired and grateful. 'Oh, thanks, Jess,' she sighed. 'That would be lovely.'

'Promise to come downstairs in a min and watch that antiques programme?' said Jess. 'You've had a horrible weekend and you've done enough for one day.'

Mum looked around at her scattered paperwork. 'You may be right,' she said. 'All this stuff, it does my head in.' Shelves and shelves of bulging files loomed down at her. She dropped her head into her hands for a moment.

'Leave it, Mum,' said Jess gently. 'You're not responsible for everything that happens in the world. It's not your fault the ozone layer's thinning or whatever. You're not going off every morning and hacking down the rainforest in person. If everyone in the world was as conscientious as you it would be a brilliant place. Give yourself a break and come downstairs. You know how you love antiques. It must be such a relief to spend an hour looking at things that are much, much older than you.'

Mum laughed. It was a tired, pale laugh, but a laugh all the same. She hauled herself to her feet. 'You're a good girl, Jess,' she said, and gave her a hug.

Jess looked over her mother's shoulder at the wall. There were places where the awful old green wallpaper was peeling right off. Mentally she stripped off the paper, dismantled the shelves, painted the room white and installed Dad in there. It was a vast improvement.

Halfway through a Very Important Teapot on the antiques show, Jess's phone pinged.

A text from Fred! Her heart jumped for joy. SKYPE NOW?

'Eight hundred pounds for a teapot?' Granny marvelled. 'I wouldn't give you five quid for it! The handle's shaped like a twig! You couldn't even grab hold of it properly!'

'I'm just going upstairs,' Jess said and left the room, trying to look leisurely and unfussed.

Once in her room, however, she flipped open her laptop with a thudding heart. She signed into Skype, and there was Fred, looking rather foggy for some reason. Her own face ballooned back at her in the small window. There were still streaks of paint in her hair.

'Fred!' she said urgently. 'Stop sitting with your back to the light! I can't see you!'

'Some people would say that was an advantage,' quipped Fred. But he moved the laptop and sat at a different angle. Jess could see the horror-film posters on his bedroom wall.

'So . . . ?' she asked. 'Tell me all about it.'

'Well, it began with the big bang, obviously,' said Fred. 'And then there was evolution – unless you're a creationist, in which case God made the world in six days, which you have to admit is good going, and –'

'No, no!' Jess interrupted. 'I mean Jodie dumping you.'

'Let's face it,' Fred admitted, 'I was born to be dumped. You were the first. You can be proud of that. It was a five-star dumping. I cried for weeks. I slept in filth.'

'You always sleep in filth. I can see it from here.' Jess's heart was racing. 'But why did she dump you? Did somebody say something about Saturday?'

'No, no,' said Fred hastily. 'She just got tired of me, I think. Lurve turned to loathing. You know how it is.'

'No, *really*,' said Jess, laughing but seriously intrigued. 'What did she say?'

'She said she thought we weren't very well suited,' said Fred. 'She said I was a pain in the neck. Now we're Just Bad Friends, apparently.'

'Well,' said Jess, marvelling. 'How amazing! Who'd have thought it?'

At this moment Jess's mobile started to ring. The caller ID showed Jodie. Jess's heart leapt in alarm.

'Agh!' Jess cried. 'It's her! I have to close my laptop! I can't talk to her with you staring at me!' She slammed the laptop shut and picked up the call. 'Hi, Jodie!' she exclaimed, trying to sound normal and breezy. 'How's it going?'

'Listen, Jess.' Jodie sounded serious and focused. 'This is just a quick call to say I've dumped Fred.'

'You've dumped Fred?' Jess tried to sound incredulous, but her words came out in a weird faux shriek.

'Yes. When you were both here this afternoon I finally realised you two are just made for each other.

It was stupid of me to try and grab a piece of the action.'

'Jodie! You've got as much right –'

'No, no! I can't talk for long now – my parents have just got home. I just wanted to explain that I'm fine about it. Lying here with my poor leg busted, I've realised a lot of things. Fred and I were so wrong together and I just wanted to tell you myself.'

'Well, thanks.' Jess could hardly think what to say. 'But that doesn't necessarily mean that Fred and I will get back together again.' She was lying through her teeth when she said this, but she didn't want to offend Jodie with a whoop of triumph. There had to be just a touch of decorum about this.

'Of course you will, you idiot!' yelled Jodie. 'You're mad about each other! Any fool can see that – even yours truly! And if you don't get back together again right away, I'll have been through all this for nothing and I shall have my revenge in this world or the next!'

Chapter 34

Jess and Fred decided to meet on Sunday, after the half-marathon.

'I don't want to see you on your own till Sunday,' said Jess, back on Skype five minutes later.

'Why Sunday?' asked Fred. 'Why wait? Why don't I run over to your place right now, sweep you up into my arms and break my back?'

'There has to be a brief period of mourning,' said Jess.

'Mourning for what?'

'Respect for Jodie.'

'I respect Jodie more than I can say,' explained Fred ruefully. 'Her shouting can crack wine glasses in faraway Winchester.'

'No, listen, Fred. She's been really generous. She's got qualities I never suspected. She's done something I could never do.'

'What?'

'Dump you for generous and kind reasons. I admit I dumped you, but that was because you were a nincompoop.'

'A spineless, gutless, irritating slob,' Fred added. 'A filthy, hideous, cowardly, farting old nincompoop.'

'And that's putting it mildly,' agreed Jess.

'But you're still prepared to see me?'

'I'll meet you on your own, in the park, by the bandstand, on Sunday at two p.m.,' said Jess. 'Think of it as a first blind date between strangers.'

'It would definitely be a help if any date involving you was blind.' Fred smiled. 'Although the streaks of blue paint in your hair do give you a certain charm.'

'We've only got a few days at school and the half-marathon on Saturday to get through. I may nod to you, I may even speak to you and, on Saturday when I'm wearing my dog costume, if you're really lucky I might widdle on your leg. But I just want to keep focused on this half-marathon thing now. I need to get some sponsors and I need to train in the few days I've got left. I know Flora and I will only be walking it, but thirteen miles is thirteen miles.'

'Fair enough.' Fred nodded. 'I'll more or less ignore

you till Sunday, then. Fantastic! I love ignoring people, especially you. I can hardly wait.'

'You can start ignoring me now,' said Jess. 'Goodbye!' And she terminated the conversation with skittish suddenness, shutting the laptop.

Suddenly the world seemed quite wonderful. Somehow she arrived downstairs, though she couldn't remember her feet touching the carpet.

Granny was just coming out of her room. Evidently the antiques programme had finished. She could hear Mum messing about in the kitchen, presumably trying to coax a few random veg into something resembling nourishment.

'Granny!' exclaimed Jess. 'You look fab! Have I seen those earrings before? They are uber cool!' She swept Granny into her arms and kissed her. Granny looked startled and, though she accepted the hug, she didn't seem all that comfortable.

'You're going to be really cross with me, Jess, I'm afraid,' she said, looking guilty.

'What?' Jess couldn't imagine being cross ever again in her whole life. 'Why?'

'That envelope with my funeral money . . . I've just found it at the bottom of my chest of drawers under my nighties.'

'You mean it wasn't in your bedside drawer after all?'

'No. I do move it about, mind you. I don't think you should stash your valuables in the same place all the time in case burglars are casing the joint.' Granny had watched too many crime movies. 'I think I must've put it there before we went away to see Jane, and I was so upset when we got back I forgot about it.'

'So the gatecrashers didn't steal your muns after all?' Jess was mightily relieved.

'Nobody did,' admitted Granny. 'And I feel really embarrassed about making such a fuss over nothing.'

'Forget it, Granno!' beamed Jess. 'I already have! Let's go and see if Mum has plans to poison us with something truly delicious tonight!'

Jess threw her arm around Granny and they headed for the kitchen.

'Mumsie!' Jess beamed. 'What's for sups tonight? If it's anything less than a full medieval banquet, I'm just not interested. Let's get fish and chips instead.'

Mum looked at Jess and faltered. She was holding a couple of droopy leeks and a massive root vegetable of some kind, adorned with roots, hairs, warts and dried mud. A vegetable soup was clearly a terrible possibility.

'Are you all right, Jess?' asked Mum. 'You look a bit, well, odd.'

'I'm happy, Mummo!' Jess burst out laughing. 'I'm just not being a miserable old bag for the first time for weeks!'

'Oh!' exclaimed Granny eagerly. 'Have you made it up with Fred again?' She didn't miss much, the beady-eyed old bloodhound.

'We're meeting up on Sunday,' announced Jess. 'After the half-marathon. We both need to focus on that first.' She sounded tremendously mature delivering this news. 'We're meeting in the park on Sunday afternoon.'

'Why not the morning?' asked Granny. 'I'd have thought you'd be up with the lark.'

'I'm going to have a ginormous lie-in on Sunday morning, Granno!' cried Jess. 'I'll have done thirteen miles the previous day and I'm not getting out of bed before twelve for anyone or anything!'

'I think it's a good idea to get fish and chips,' said Mum, avoiding an emotional conversation in her usual practical way. Dad was the one who would hurl confetti about and scream with joy when he heard the news. 'And, as a special celebration, you may also have mushy peas.'

*

The next few days were spent training for the half-marathon. Jess and Flora walked round and round the park for hours. Flora's family was fairly dog-friendly so she had a range of old leads to test out the dog-on-a-lead idea with. They chose an extending one for comfort. And Jess bought a stylish black collar with studs and bags of attitude. The man in the pet shop looked rather startled when she tried it on, but he obviously wasn't the father of teenagers.

Sponsorship proved easy. Jess and Flora just sent emails to everybody on their contact lists and people were surprisingly generous, though most of them did insist on having photos of Jess in her dog suit in return.

Phil sent her a wonderful costume, so that on the morning of the race, Jess only had to dive into it and do up a couple of zips, and she was transformed into a large white poodle. She bounded around the house and begged for biscuits.

The half-marathon turned out to be amazing. Fred was wearing a T-shirt which read *CANCER RESEARCH* on the front and *SAVE THE LIBRARY* on the back.

'There's still room on my backside if anyone wants to advertise anything,' he quipped.

Jess was touched that he'd shown his support for her mum, though she wasn't able to express her thanks properly, partly because they were still in their casual, half-ignoring-each-other mode, and partly because she was dressed as an enormous white poodle.

Once the half-marathon started, she and Flora were at the back, miles behind the main pack of runners, together with some other people in fancy dress, including one guy who had come as a tortoise and somebody disguised as a Dalek. Unless, of course, it was a real Dalek. Sometimes it's hard to tell.

Jess and Flora had the best time. Occasionally Jess would lift her leg against a lamp post, which always made the watching crowds roar with laughter. Once they got past ten miles, Jess's legs were aching terribly and she was exhausted, but they managed to finish the course.

Jodie, who was having her first day out on crutches, met them at the finish line.

'Flora, Jess, you legends!' she cried as she hugged them. 'Fred did brilliantly, too – he was forty-fifth!'

'Wow, what a high-flyer!' said Jess, ripping off her dog head. 'Phew, it was hot in there! I don't know how dogs cope in all that fur!'

'I'm going home to have a shower!' said Flora. 'And

it's going to be a marathon shower, too! How much have we raised, Jodie?'

'Nearly two thousand pounds!' beamed Jodie. 'Plus my dad's doing well on his treatment and the docs say the outlook is really, really positive!'

Jess gave Jodie another hug. She was delighted for her, and for a moment she felt close to tears. Happy tears, though. Jess could see Mum and Dad making their way towards her through the crowds, and Dad was brandishing his camera – evidently her canine triumph had been captured for posterity. Jess felt a funny surge of wobbly happiness. She was so lucky to have such great friends and a supportive family. She couldn't see Fred anywhere right now, but she knew that tomorrow they'd be meeting in the park, and she hugged this secret to herself as the best thing of all.

'Well, I'm absolutely shattered!' Jess announced with a tired grin. 'Now I'm going to crawl off to my kennel and sleep for a thousand years.'

Chapter 35

On Sunday morning, Jess woke at the crack of noon. A split second later, a flood of happiness rolled over her as she remembered that in just two hours she would be meeting Fred in the park for the first blind date of their new life.

She leapt out of bed – and screamed in pain. Every muscle in her body was in agony. The half-marathon had pushed her to her limit, even though she'd been only walking. She hadn't had enough time to train for it properly, either. Never mind. She would get to the park even if she had to crawl.

Thank goodness she could apply make-up sitting down. She spent ages on her eyebrows alone. Somehow they had to radiate wit, verve and panache. The right one was OK, but the left one was short on verve. Jess was driven to the brink of insanity by the impossibility of injecting verve with just tweezers and pencil. Why had God put humankind on the planet in order to torment them with the impossibility of matching eyebrows? On the other hand, if Homo sapiens had just evolved, why hadn't those with uneven eyebrows died out as miserable outcasts?

Working on her lips half an hour later, Jess mused wryly that Fred didn't like girls wearing make-up anyway. Besides, he'd already seen her looking quite frightful on a number of occasions and yet he was still, it seemed, intrigued by the idea of meeting her in the park. The make-up session was for herself. It was a celebration thing.

Finally, Jess was ready. After ingesting a brunch of French toast, she set off towards the park, hobbling.

With every muscle in her legs as stiff as a board, Jess couldn't float along the pavement in the way she would have liked. She had to limp and shuffle in an unattractive hunched-up way. She began to fear she was going to be late. Being late would be OK if she was able to shimmy elegantly towards Fred on a cloud of glamour, being marvellous. But to turn up hobbling, panting and puffing wasn't the entrance Jess had been dreaming of.

As she entered the park and approached the

bandstand, she could see a distant figure. He was so far away she couldn't be absolutely sure it was Fred. It was a tall figure, slightly stooping. Perhaps it wasn't Fred – perhaps it was an old man. But as they got nearer, Jess could see that it was indeed Fred. She recognised his grey hoodie and his air of thoughtfulness. He was really hobbling, too – hobbling and limping.

If this had been the last minute of a slushy romantic movie, they'd have run into each other's arms in beautiful slow motion. Jess's hair, which would have been long and shiny, would have been streaming behind her in the wind like an ad for shampoo. Fred would have been brooding and masterful, and would have covered the space between them in five effortless bounds. This meeting was going to fall far short of the romantic cliché.

As they got within shouting distance, Jess noticed that Fred was wearing a backpack and that something was sticking out of it. She hoped he wasn't going to suggest an elopement. After all, this was their first date.

'I can hardly move!' called Fred. 'But I've heroically forced myself to hobble here!'

'Me too! My legs will have to be removed and replaced with a skateboard!' replied Jess.

As they both neared the bandstand, Jess realised

that the thing sticking out of Fred's rucksack was a head. Not a human head – Granny would be disappointed – but a bear's head. And not just any old bear. Rasputin! Rasputin was peeping out of Fred's rucksack and kind of looking over his shoulder like a very bad-tempered baby.

'Rasputin!' screamed Jess in rapture.

'I knew you'd ignore me once you caught sight of the bear,' grumbled Fred. 'It's a bit much being upstaged by a soft toy.'

'Rasputin! Rasputin!' Jess was ecstatic. She scrabbled about in Fred's rucksack, undoing the toggles, and finally managed to pull Rasputin out and cover him with kisses. 'How did you find him?' she asked, burying her face in his lovely old fur, where so many of her tears had been shed. 'However did you manage to find him?'

'I've been making enquiries,' said Fred. 'One likes to be of service.' He looked down at her with softly shining eyes.

'One has succeeded,' whispered Jess, gratefulness and love surging through her every vein.

'So . . .' Fred stood there awkwardly. 'Are you . . .' He pulled a piece of paper out of his pocket. 'Are you Girl, 16, Charming But Insane?'

'Are you Lanky Nincompoop With No Spine And Feet That Are Far From Fragrant?'

'I admit it!' Fred held out his hand. 'How very, very delightful to meet you at last.'

Jess took his hand and shook it, as if they were strangers formally meeting for the first time.

'How do you do?' said Jess, smiling not just with her lips but with her whole body. Even her big toes were smiling.

'So . . .' Fred hesitated. 'Miss, er . . .' He consulted his scrap of paper. 'Sorry, I've forgotten your name, but would you like a coffee?'

'I'd like nothing more,' said Jess.

He offered her his arm, like a gentleman out of a Jane Austen novel, and she took it, and they hobbled off together into what should have been a sunset, but which was only a rather grey English afternoon in late spring. Birds were singing and a light rain was beginning to fall, and Jess knew she would always remember this moment as perfect, even if she lived to be a hundred.

Win a Totally Cool Purple iPad 2

To be in with a chance of winning, all you need to do is answer the following question correctly.

The name of Jess's best friend is . . .
a) Flora
b) Fiona
c) Felicity

Email your answer to
childrensmarketing@bloomsbury.com
or visit **www.JessJordan.co.uk**!*

Hi, guys!

You're so brilliant reading this and it's really cheered me up, as Fred is being a bit of a toad at the moment — not that he's covered with warts and is shooting poison out of his neck (but give him time). Sometimes I feel that you're my only friend, especially when Flora's at orchestra practice. So please, please, do me a ginormous favour and visit my fabulous, dazzling, low-calorie, high energy website — **www.JessJordan.co.uk**!!!!

I'm going to be blogging away (I wrote glogging by accident at first and I kind of like it, so I might be glogging too) and I can promise you loads of laughs, polls, quizzes, interactive stuff, downloadable goodies, plus sensational secrets that Fred, Flora, Ben, Mackenzie and Jodie have begged me never to reveal! Don't tell them I sent you — and promise you'll be there!

Love,
Jess

Jess Jordan's Top Tips on How to Handle an Unexpected Party

Shout out, 'Who's for tinned rice pudding?'

If they still won't leave, announce that the Bishop of Boringfield is coming to deliver one of his lovely sermons.

Gather up all the stinky old bits of leftover cheese in the fridge and place them on the hottest radiator.

Hide the disco music and replace it with Beetroothoven's *Funeral March with Extra Glooms*.

If all else fails, don a false moustache and go to live in China.

For more top tips from Jess, visit **www.JessJordan.co.uk**

Just in case you missed

Charming But Insane,

read on for a spectacularly amazing extract!

Chapter 1

Eyes, nose, lips. Jess was drawing a face on her hand. She should have been making notes for her history essay: a list of 'Reasons Why King Charles I Was Unpopular'. But instead she was giving herself a love-tattoo of the beautiful Ben Jones. The flicked-up hair, the slanty grin . . . Oh no! It didn't look like Ben Jones at all. It looked like a demented iguana.

Art wasn't Jess's strong point. She wrote, *Ben Jones, – or Demented Iguana?* under her tattoo, and coughed in a signal to her friend Flora that communication was desired. It was a kind of ringtone. Flora looked up and Jess held the tattoo up to her. Flora smiled, but it was a kind of pretend smile, and immediately afterwards Flora glanced furtively at Miss Dingle and dived straight back into her work.

Miss Dingle – Dingbat to her fans – was glaring

from the teacher's desk. 'Jess Jordan! What's your problem?'

'Oh, Miss, there are so many,' sighed Jess, hastily pulling her sleeve down to hide the portrait-tattoo of Ben Jones: the Demented Iguana. 'Tragic broken home, hideous genetic inheritance . . . massive bum . . .' A few people giggled.

'Get on with your work,' snapped Miss Dingle, trying to sound steely and terrifying, even though she had a weedy little voice and a tendency to spit. 'If you showed half as much interest in writing history projects as you do in trying to be amusing, you'd be the star pupil instead of the class dunce.'

Everybody hid their faces in their books and cracked up – as silently as possible, of course. The whole room shook.

'And the rest of you!' shouted Miss Dingle. 'Be quiet and get on with writing your list of reasons – unless you all want to stay behind after school! I'm quite tempted to put the whole group in detention!' At the word 'detention', another drop of spit went sailing across the room.

There was a muffled explosion as everyone tried to avoid laughing out loud by eating their own tonsils, but frenzied scribbling was also resumed. Nobody wanted to stay behind after school. Jess picked up her dictionary and tried to look intelligent. She turned the pages, hoping for a rude word. Suddenly she had an idea. Hey! Maybe you could consult the dictionary, a bit like the Tarot. Think of a question, then open it at random. Jess closed her eyes and concentrated. *Will Ben Jones and I ever be an item?*

Her finger jabbed at a word. *Parsley. A well-known garden herb, used for flavouring soup.* Well, not a brilliant result, obviously. But maybe there was a hidden meaning. Perhaps you could make a boy fall in love with you by rubbing parsley behind your ears, or sprinkling chopped parsley in his pants while he was swimming.

Jess suddenly caught Dingbat's eye again. A dangerous moment. Hastily Jess copied down the title of the history essay. 'Reasons Why King Charles I Was Unpopular.' All she had to do was read chapter six of the history book. Jess flicked through the book and looked at the pictures. Charles I had sad, haunted eyes and a stylish goatee. Flora had told her that he had been only about five feet tall. Some kind of Hobbit, obviously. And then he had had his head chopped off – pretty bad news for anybody of course, but for a short guy clearly a disaster, stylewise.

'Reasons Why King Charles I Was Unpopular.' Jess looked across at Flora, who was writing so hard that her whole body was shaking. She had written three whole pages already, and if Jess was going to catch up with her, she had to make a start. Jess picked up her pen and let her imagination run away with her. This was always dangerous.

Reasons Why King Charles I Was Unpopular
1. He never changed his pants.
2. He refused to grow.
3. He passed a law saying everybody taller than him had to have their legs cut off.
4. He slurped his soup.
5. He used to bottle his farts and sell them to the tourists.

Somehow, at this point, Jess's inspiration dried up and she began to think about Ben Jones again. She formed a plan to steal a bit of DNA from his football boots or a hair from the shoulder of his blazer. There would be instructions somewhere on the internet, so she ought to be able to genetically engineer a Ben Jones look-alike, in case the real one proved unavailable. She gazed in adoration at the tattoo of Ben Jones: the

Demented Iguana. How she longed to have his babies. Or possibly lay his eggs.

Jess started another list: 'Reasons Why Ben Jones Is Popular.' This was much easier than the history list.

1. Hair like golden grass (if only I could picnic on it).
2. Eyes blue enough to swim in (he's beginning to sound like a holiday destination).
3. A cute, slow, slanty smile that could defrost Antarctica.
4. Doesn't speak much, i.e. not loud and trashy, and . . .
5. Oozes mystery and charisma.

Suddenly, the bell rang. A massive sigh of relief spread through the room. Everybody put down their pens, yawned and stretched. Tiffany, a plump, dark-haired girl with savage eyebrows, turned round to Jess and hissed, 'Don't forget my party tomorrow night! Be there or else!'

'Sure,' said Jess. 'I was gonna stay in and darn some divine socks, but for you – I'll make that major sacrifice.' Tiffany's family was quite rich – at least, by Jess's standards – and Jess was quite looking forward to quaffing champagne and swinging from the chandeliers.

Jess's best friend, the goddess Flora, was the only person in the class who hadn't finished working yet. She scribbled away harder than ever, her golden hair glittering. One grain of her divine dandruff could make the blind see again, and revive small insects that had been trodden on.

Flora finished off her sentence with a flourish, tossed back her hair with a great flash of supernatural light, turned to Jess and grinned. *It's a good job the beautiful, over-achieving glamour puss is my best friend*, thought Jess, *or I might just have to kill her.*

'Jess Jordan!' thundered Miss Dingle in her tiny fairy's voice, above the noise of people packing up their bags. 'Will you come up here and show me your list of reasons, please!'

Get to Know Sue Limb!

The first thing Sue ever wrote was the letter 'S' and it's still her favourite letter. As a toddler she wrote on walls, but at school she was given exercise books and filled them with stories of children who lived alone on islands and had adventures with boats and dogs. Though a tomboy, Sue was also a coward and deeply scared of boats, dogs, islands and adventures, but she discovered that writing was a way of experiencing other lives while keeping your feet dry.

As a teenager she realised that if you could make people laugh they didn't notice how nerdy you were. Sue found that comedy was a way of dealing with the bad stuff that happens in life, such as embarrassment and anxiety. Despite her love of comedy and writing, she ignored these hints from the universe and briefly attempted to be a teacher. Sue hates imposing her will on other people (even her dog had to teach himself to sit and fetch) so her days in the schoolroom were numbered and she escaped from the Ministry of Education.

Writing for young people has always been a big part of Sue's working life, mainly because she still doesn't feel grown up. In recent years she has produced the Jess Jordan books and revisited her early childhood in the *Ruby Rogers* series.

Sue lives in a wild, rocky and remote part of Gloucestershire, on a farm, and when not writing she likes to be out of doors messing about with plants and animals.

A Few More
Facts about Sue!

✻ **Name:** Sue Limb.

✻ **Star sign:** Virgo.

✻ **Favourite colour:** Green.

✻ **Favourite number:** Seven.

✻ **Favourite thing to do:** Give my dog a bath.

✻ **Favourite food:** Anything with pesto.

✻ **Where were you born?** Hitchin, Hertfordshire, England.

✻ **Where do you live now?** On a remote farm in Gloucestershire.

* **What were you like at school?** A tomboy-ish nerd.

* **Have you got brothers and sisters?** One older brother, who's a jazz musician.

* **What did you want to be as a child?** Secretary-General of the United Nations (I told you I was a nerd).

* **How did you start writing?** At age two, I liked doodling the letter 'S'. When I grew up, I tried teaching, couldn't cope, and writing seemed to be the only thing possible.

* **What did you do before you were a writer?** I was a teacher, screaming in vain for quiet while my classes rioted gently around me.

* **Where do you write?** Anywhere – I particularly like writing on trains. But when I'm at home, in a room with windows opening into a wild wood.

* **What was your favourite book as a child?** *The Railway Children* by E. Nesbit.

✳ **What's your favourite children's book now?** *Where the Wild Things Are* by Maurice Sendak.

✳ **What's your favourite adult book?** *Persuasion* by Jane Austen.

✳ **What tips do you have for budding writers?** Read a lot!

✳ **What's your favourite TV programme?** *Frasier*.

✳ **What makes you laugh?** Harry Enfield and Paul Whitehouse as the Surgeons.

✳ **What's your favourite movie?** *Some Like It Hot*.

✳ **Who do you imagine playing Jess, Flora and Fred in a movie?** Carey Mulligan would be Jess, Emma Watson would be Flora and Jamie Campbell Bower would be Fred.